Death by Pantyhose

Books by Laura Levine

THIS PEN FOR HIRE

LAST WRITES

KILLER BLONDE

SHOES TO DIE FOR

THE PMS MURDER

DEATH BY PANTYHOSE

Published by Kensington Publishing Corporation

A Jaine Austen Mystery

Death by Pantyhose

Laura Levine

KENSINGTON BOOKS
http://www.kensingtonbooks.com

KENSINGTON BOOKS are published by

Kensington Publishing Corp.
850 Third Avenue
New York, NY 10022

All Kensington titles, imprints, and distributed lines are available at special quantity discounts for bulk purchases for sales promotion, premiums, fund-raising, educational, or institutional use.

Special book excerpts or customized printings can also be created to fit specific needs. For details, write or phone the office of the Kensington Special Sales Manager: Attn. Special Sales Department. Kensington Publishing Corp., 850 Third Avenue, New York, NY 10022. Phone: 1-800-221-2647.

Kensington and the K logo Reg. U.S. Pat. & TM Off.

Library of Congress Card Catalogue Number: 2006939880
ISBN-13: 978-0-7582-0785-2
ISBN-10: 0-7582-0785-9

First Printing: June 2007
10 9 8 7 6 5 4 3 2 1

Printed in the United States of America

In loving memory of Mr. Guy,
the sweetest guy in "Guy Land."

ACKNOWLEDGMENTS

I'm so grateful, as always, to my editor John Scognamiglio and my agent Evan Marshall for their valued guidance and support. Thanks to Hiro Kimura for his nifty cover art. And to Joanne Fluke, who takes time out from writing her own bestselling Hannah Swensen mysteries to share her insights and her brownies. A special thanks to the wonderful readers who've taken the time to write me. And to my friends and family for putting up with me while I'm wrangling with a plot. And to all of you who've battled Los Angeles traffic to show up at my book signings, I owe you one!

Finally, a loving thanks to my most loyal fan and ardent supporter, my husband Mark.

Chapter 1

Ever have one of those days where everything seems to go your way, where the gods smile on your every move and good luck follows you around like an eager puppy?

Neither have I.

No matter how great things start out in my life, sooner or later something is guaranteed to hit the fan.

Take the day the whole pantyhose mess began. It started out smoothly enough. My cat, Prozac, waited until the civilized hour of 8 A.M. before swan diving on my chest to wake me up.

"Morning, pumpkin," I murmured, as she nuzzled her furry head under my chin.

She looked at me with big green eyes that seemed to say, *You're my favorite human in all the world.* (Well, not exactly. What they really seemed to say was, *When do we eat?* But I knew deep down, she loved me.)

When I looked out the window, I was happy to see that the early morning fog that hovers over L.A. for months on end had finally taken a powder. The sun was back in action, shining its little heart out.

Things got even better when I discovered a free sample of Honey Nutty Raisin Bits with my morning newspaper, which meant I didn't have to nuke one of the petrified Pop-Tarts in my freezer for breakfast.

After feeding Prozac a bowl of Moist Mackerel Guts and inhaling my Honey Nutty Raisin Bits straight from the box, I did the crossword puzzle (with nary a trip to the dictionary) and spent the rest of the morning polishing my resume for an upcoming job interview. And not just any job interview. I, Jaine Austen, a gal who normally writes toilet bowl ads for a living, had a meeting lined up that very morning at Rubin-McCormick, one of L.A.'s hottest ad agencies.

And so it was with a spring in my step and Honey Nutty Raisin Bits on my breath that I headed off to the bedroom to get dressed for my interview. I took out my one and only Prada suit from my closet, pristine clean in its dry-cleaning bag. No unsightly ketchup stains ambushed me at the last minute, like they usually do. I checked my one and only pair of Manolo Blahnik shoes. Not a scuff mark in sight. I checked my hair in the mirror. No crazy cowlicks or brillo patches in my natural curls. Like I said, the gods were smiling on me.

And that's when I saw it: a zit on my chin the size of a small Aleutian island.

Now I've got nothing against the Aleutian Islands. I'm sure they're quite scenic. But not on my chin, s'il vous plaît.

I was surveying the disaster in the mirror when the phone rang. I let the machine get it.

Hi! A woman's eager voice came on the line. *I saw your ad in the Yellow Pages, and I'm calling to see if you write comedy material. I'm a stand-up comic, and everyone says I'm hilarious.*

Uh-oh. My Bad Job Antenna sprang into action. People who say they're hilarious are usually about as funny as left-over meatloaf.

I need someone to write some new jokes for my act. Your ad said your rates were reasonable. I sure hope so. I was think-

ing maybe five bucks a joke. Six or seven if they're really funny.

Five bucks a joke? Was she kidding? Court jesters were making more than that in the Middle Ages.

Give me a call if you're interested. My name is Dorcas. Oh, and by the way, you can catch my act at the Laff Palace on open-mike nights. I'm the one who throws my pantyhose into the audience.

Did I hear right? Did she actually say she threw her pantyhose into the audience? Sounded more like a stripper than a comic to me.

Needless to say, I didn't write down her number. In the first place, I wasn't really a comedy writer. And in the second place, even if I was a comedy writer, the last thing I wanted to do was write jokes for a pantyhose-tossing comic. And in the third and most important place, for once in my life, I wasn't desperate for money.

Yes, for the past several months, my computer had been practically ablaze with writing assignments: I'd done a freelance piece for the *L.A. Times* on 24-hour Botox Centers. A new brochure for Mel's Mufflers (*Our Business Is Exhausting*). And to top it off, I'd just finished an extensive ad campaign for my biggest client, Toiletmasters Plumbers, introducing their newest product, an extra large toilet bowl called Big John. All of which meant I had actual funds in my checking account.

What's more, if my job interview today went well, I'd be bringing home big bucks from the Rubin-McCormick ad agency. I'd answered their ad for a freelance writer, and much to my surprise Stan McCormick himself had called me to set up an appointment. Who knows? Maybe he'd seen my botox piece in the *L.A. Times.* Or maybe he was the proud owner of a Big John. I didn't care why he wanted to see me; all I knew was that I had a shot at a job at one of L.A.'s premiere ad agencies.

Which was why that zit on my chin was so annoying. But with diligent effort (and enough concealer to caulk a bathtub), I eventually managed to camouflage it.

After I finished dressing, I surveyed myself in the mirror. If I do say so myself, I looked nifty. My Prada suit pared inches from my hips (which needed all the paring they could get). My Manolos gave me three extra statuesque inches. And my frizz-free hair was a veritable shinefest.

I headed out to the living room, where I found Prozac draped over the back of the sofa.

"Wish me luck, Pro," I said, as I bent down to kiss her good-bye.

She yawned in my face, blasting me with mackerel breath.

Hurry back. I may want a snack.

"I love you, too, dollface."

Then I headed outside to my Corolla, where the birds were chirping, the sun was shining, and the grass was growing greener by the minute.

Nothing, I thought, could possibly go wrong on such a spectacular day.

I'm sure the gods had a hearty chuckle over that one.

Chapter 2

The Rubin-McCormick Agency was headquartered in a high-rent business complex in Santa Monica, a gleaming Mediterranean extravaganza with swaying palm trees and waterfalls out front. If you didn't know it was an office building, you'd swear you were at a Ritz-Carlton. I drove past the waterfalls to the impeccably landscaped parking lot, thrilled to have landed an interview in such august surroundings.

The lobby was deserted when I got there. It was nearly eleven, that quiet time before the lunch rush, and I had the place all to myself. I rang for the elevator and started rehearsing my opening greeting.

"Hello, Mr. McCormick," I said to the elevator doors. "I'm Jaine Austen."

Nah. Maybe "Mr." was too formal. These ad agencies were hip, happening places.

"Hey, Stan. Jaine here."

No, no, no! That was way too familiar. I wanted to be his writer, not his golf buddy.

"A pleasure to meet you, Mr. McCormick," I tried. "I'm Jaine Austen."

Suddenly a voice came out of nowhere.

"A pleasure to meet you, too, Ms. Austen."

I whirled around and saw a tall guy in his late forties,

graying at the temples, in khakis and a cashmere blazer. He wore tinted aviator glasses and carried an attaché case that cost more than my Corolla.

Dear Lord, I prayed. *Please don't let him be Stan McCormick.*

He smiled a craggy suntanned smile.

"Hi. I'm Stan McCormick."

Great. My would-be employer saw me talking to myself. Just the impression I was going for. The Recently Released Mental Patient Look.

The elevator, which had taken its sweet time showing up, finally dinged open, and we both got on.

"This is so embarrassing," I said. "Not exactly the way I was hoping to start my interview."

"Interview?" He blinked, puzzled.

"I have an appointment to meet with you at eleven this morning."

He still looked puzzled.

"I answered your ad for a freelance writer. Remember?"

"Damn," he said, slapping his forehead with his open palm. "Now look who's embarrassed. I forgot all about it. Completely slipped my mind. I've been down in Newport all morning with a client."

The elevator doors opened onto the Rubin-McCormick reception area, a stark white expanse with nothing on the walls except the Rubin-McCormick logo. A cool, blond receptionist fielded phone calls behind a wraparound desk.

"Actually," he said, waving to the receptionist, "I'm starving. How about I take you to Westwood Gardens and we have our interview over an early lunch?"

My spirits perked up. Lunch—along with breakfast, dinner, and brunch—happens to be one of my favorite meals. What's more, he was taking me to Westwood Gardens, one of the best restaurants in town.

"Sounds wonderful," I said, as we started back down to the lobby.

"Mind if we take your car?" he asked. "I just dropped mine off with the valets to be detailed."

Drat. I'd sweated bullets putting together my Prada–Manolo Blahnik ensemble, hoping to pass myself off as an A-list writer. What would he think when he saw my geriatric Corolla, littered with McDonald's ketchup packets?

"I don't mind," I lied. "Not at all."

We headed over to my dusty Corolla, which I saw, to my dismay, was sporting a big white blob on the windshield, a love note from a bird with a serious gastrointestinal disorder.

"Excuse my car," I said, as we got in. "I'm afraid it's a mess."

"No, no. It's fine," he said, plucking an Almond Joy wrapper from the passenger seat before he sat down.

I gritted my teeth in annoyance. Why the heck hadn't I washed the car before the interview?

I turned on my new state-of-the-art stereo system, a gift I'd bought myself with my Big John earnings, hoping Stan would be so impressed with the quality of the sound, he wouldn't notice the Big Gulp Slurpee cup at his feet.

And he did seem impressed.

"Great speakers," he said, "for such a crummy car."

Okay, so he didn't say the part about the crummy car, but it had to have been on his mind.

It was a short drive to Westwood Gardens, most of which we spent making small talk and staring at the bird poop on the windshield.

I pulled up to the restaurant and handed the Corolla over to a valet. Normally I'd circle the block seventeen times looking for a parking space before springing for a valet, but I didn't want to seem like a piker, especially when Stan said, "Don't worry about the valet, Jaine. I'll take care of him."

I handed my keys to the valet and we headed inside.

Westwood Gardens is an upscale eatery with exposed brick walls, flagstone floors, and rustic wrought-iron furniture. Very "My Year in Provence." A reed-thin hostess/actress seated us at a cozy table for two by the window, overlooking the bustling Westwood street scene. Sizing up Stan as someone who could possibly give her a part in a play/movie/commercial, she shot him a dazzling smile and drifted off.

"So," Stan said, after we'd looked through our menus, "what looks good to you?"

Now this was a tricky question. What looked good to me was the steak sandwich with onion rings and thick-cut fries. But I couldn't possibly allow myself to order it. I had an image to uphold. Women in Prada and Manolos simply do not order dishes that come with ketchup and A1 sauce. Women in Prada and Manolos order dainty salads made of arugula and endive and other stuff I usually don't touch with a ten-foot fork.

"I'll have the chopped salad," I said, with a sigh.

"Is that all?" Stan asked. "I'm going to have the steak sandwich. It's fantastic. You really should get it, too."

"But it's an awful lot to eat," I demurred.

Yeah, right. If he could only see me alone in my apartment plowing my way through a pepperoni pizza.

"Oh, go on," he urged. "You only go round once, right?"

"Well, if you insist." I felt like throwing my arms around the guy and kissing him. "One steak sandwich it is."

At which point, a stunning actor/waiter sidled up to our table. Like the hostess, he shot Stan a high-wattage smile. Something about Stan simply radiated importance. I, on the other hand, in spite of my Prada and Manolos, wasn't fooling anybody. The gang here at the Gardens instinctively knew me for the poseur that I was.

"Hi, I'm Phineas," the waiter said, still beaming at Stan, "and I'll be your server today." He reeled off the list of Today's

Specials with all the intensity of Hamlet yakking at Yorick's skull.

"We'll have two steak sandwiches," Stan said when he was through.

"Wonderful choice!" Phineas gushed.

"And how about we split a tiramisu for dessert?" Stan said to me.

Was this the boss from heaven, or what?

"Sounds great!"

Phineas whisked off to get our food, barely restraining himself from leaving a head shot and resume in Stan's lap.

"So," Stan said when he was gone, "tell me about yourself, Jaine."

I put on my tap shoes and launched into my usual spiel, telling him about the work I'd done for Toiletmasters (*In a Rush to Flush? Call Toiletmasters!*), Ackerman's Awnings (*Just a Shade Better*), and Tip Top Dry Cleaners (*We Clean for You. We Press for You. We Even Dye for You.*) I wished I had classier accounts to talk about, but Stan seemed interested.

After a while, Phineas showed up with our steak sandwiches. We devoured them with gusto, and afterwards, Stan looked through my book of writing samples. When he was finished, he shut the book and popped the last of his fries in his mouth.

"Frankly, Jaine, I was looking for someone with a bit more experience on national accounts."

My heart sank. Oh, well. I had to look on the bright side. At least I got a steak sandwich out of the deal.

"On the other hand," he said, grinning, "I like the way you write."

He liked the way I wrote! Maybe I had a shot at this gig, after all.

"So the job is yours if you want it."

"Oh, yes! I'd love it."

Then, just when I thought things couldn't get any more divine, Phineas showed up with what had to be the creamiest tiramisu this side of Tuscany.

"Perfect timing," Stan said. "Let's celebrate."

I picked up my fork and was just about to plunge it into the delectable confection when Stan asked, "Don't you want to know what the assignment is?"

"Oh, right. Sure. The assignment."

In my excitement over the tiramisu, it had sort of slipped my mind.

"It's a brand new product launch. I think you'll be perfect for it. I've got all the facts here in my attaché case."

He reached down to get his case and frowned.

"Damn. I must've left it in your car."

"I'll go get it," I said, shooting a wistful look at the tiramisu. I hated to leave it, but the man had just offered me a job, and the least I could do was get his attaché case.

"No," Stan said. "I'll go. You start on dessert."

Obviously he could see how much I was lusting after the tiramisu.

"Are you sure?" I asked.

"Of course. I'll be right back."

What a sweetie he was to give me first dibs on dessert. I gave him the parking ticket, and he headed for the door.

Once more, I gazed at the tiramisu in all its creamy glory. I debated about whether or not to take a bite. I really should wait until Stan got back. But he did tell me to go ahead and get started. I'd just have one teeny bite. And then we'd share the rest together.

I took a teeny bite. Okay, so it wasn't so teeny. It was a major forkful. Sheer heaven. I couldn't resist taking another. But that was it. No more. Absolutely not!

And I'm proud to say not a single morsel passed through my lips—not for three whole seconds. Then I broke down and had another bite. And another. And another. Until, to my horror, I saw that I'd eaten all but one biteful.

I was utterly ashamed of myself. What would Stan think? He'd probably take back the job offer. I'd given up a lucrative gig with Rubin-McCormick for a piece of tiramisu!

It was at that moment that I happened to glance out the window and saw the valet handing Stan the keys to my Corolla. That's funny. Stan was getting in on the driver's side of the car. Surely he'd left his attaché case on the passenger side.

It's a good thing my mouth wasn't full of tiramisu; otherwise I might have choked at what I saw next. Much to my amazement, Stan started the engine, gave a friendly wave to the valet, and drove off.

What on earth was he doing? And then it dawned on me.

Stan McCormick had just stolen my car!

Chapter 3

Of course, the man who stole my car wasn't really Stan McCormick. The man who stole my car, as the cops pointed out when they showed up at the restaurant, was an opportunistic car thief who'd pulled this let's-take-your-car-to-lunch scam many times before.

Like an idiot, I'd unwittingly given him all the information he needed. He'd overheard both my name and Stan's name while I was rehearsing in the lobby. And then, on the elevator, I'd told him I was a writer coming in for a job interview. I'd practically handed him my car keys.

The cop who wrote up the police report offered little-to-no-hope of my car being recovered.

"We'll call you if we find it," he said, "but it's probably on its way to a chop shop as we speak."

Oh, crud. That meant I was probably going to have to buy a car. Even with the money I got from my insurance company, it was still going to cost a fortune.

I might not have been strapped for cash that morning, but I was now. I needed that job with Rubin-McCormick, and I needed it badly. So as soon as the cops left, I got out my cell phone and called the real Stan McCormick.

Unfortunately, the real Stan McCormick did not believe my story about meeting the phony Stan McCormick in an elevator and driving off to lunch with him. He thought I was just another airhead who'd slept through her interview. It didn't help that I was babbling while I told it to him. (*You see, he was wearing an expensive cashmere blazer and I just assumed he was you, especially when he waved to the receptionist, and of course, he already knew your name because he'd overheard me talking to the elevator doors. . . .*)

"I would've respected you a lot more," the real Stan McCormick said, "if you'd just told the truth and admitted you screwed up."

And then, before I knew it, I was babbling to a dial tone.

I snapped my phone shut, on the verge of tears.

I guess Phineas could see how upset I was, because at that very moment, he rallied to my side with a cup of coffee and a bill for $76.23.

"I already added in the tip," he said, "in case it slipped your mind."

What a thoughtful fellow.

"Will there be anything else?" he asked.

I sure hoped not.

Ten minutes later, I was standing outside the restaurant when my best friend, Kandi Tobolowski, came roaring up in her Miata. The cops had offered to give me a lift, but I needed a shoulder to cry on, so I'd called Kandi, whose shoulder is always available for weeping and wailing.

"You poor thing!" she said, wrapping me in a hug as I sunk in the Miata. "Tell Kandi all about it."

"I will, but first, you've got to drive me over to Crazy Dave's."

"Crazy Dave's?"

"A car rental place on Pico and Cloverfield."

While waiting for Kandi to show up, I'd called my trusty

insurance company, whose motto is: *When Trouble Strikes, Don't Come Whining to Us.* The helpful claims lady told me that I was entitled to the princely sum of fifteen dollars a day to rent a car. She had to be kidding. I could barely rent a bicycle for fifteen bucks a day.

Which is why I'd decided to rent a car from Crazy Dave's Rent-A-Wreck. I'd driven past Crazy Dave's lot many times and remembered a sign out front claiming: *My Cars Are So Cheap, It's CRAZY!* The price seemed right to me.

"Okay," Kandi said, swerving out into traffic and barely missing a bus. "Now tell me everything that happened."

And I did. I told her how I ran into the phony Stan McCormick and how he figured out I was going on a job interview and stole my car and stuck me with the bill for two steak sandwiches and a tiramisu.

"I don't believe it!" she said when I was finished.

"I know. It's incredible, isn't it?"

"You had a steak sandwich and tiramisu for lunch? Do you realize how many calories you ate? Not to mention cholesterol and triglycerides."

"Kandi, I think you're missing the point. The guy stole my car. The cops said it's probably gone forever. I'm going to have to fork over money I don't have for a new one."

"Twenty years from now when your arteries are clogged with old steak sandwiches, you won't care about that silly car. And besides, the car isn't really a problem. I can give you the money to get another one."

Kandi happens to be one of the most generous women in the world. She's always offering to bail me out of my financial scrapes, but due to my idiotic pride, I'm always turning her down.

Of course, Kandi can afford to be generous—thanks to her job as a writer on the Saturday morning cartoon show *Beanie*

& the Cockroach. Yes, I know it's hard to believe that someone can make scads of money writing jokes for a household pest, but she does.

The thing is, I know Kandi would write me a check in a minute if I asked her, and I'm always touched by her generosity.

"I can't let you do that," I said. "But thanks for offering. And thanks for coming to get me. I hope I didn't drag you away from an important script meeting."

"Actually, I was auditioning actresses."

"Oh? One of your supporting insects get sick?"

"I wasn't auditioning for the show. I'm trying to find someone to play me."

"You?"

"Yes," she said, cutting in front of a BMW. "I got another speeding ticket again. Can you believe that?"

"Of course I can believe it, Kandi. You're a terrible driver. I've seen crash test dummies drive better than you."

"I am not a bad driver!" she protested, giving the finger to the BMW. "Anyhow, I need somebody to go to traffic school for me."

"Why can't you go yourself?"

"I can't. It brings back too many memories."

"What memories?"

"Have you forgotten? That's where I met Steve."

I'm ashamed to admit I had forgotten. Steve was Kandi's ex-fiancé, a darling guy who she met in traffic school; they were all set to get married when he ran off with the wedding planner—another darling guy named Armando.

"I can't possibly face traffic school again."

"Can't you take a course on-line?"

"Online, in person. It's all the same. Just thinking about those traffic rules makes me weepy. Steve and I first exchanged glances during a discussion of U-turns," she said, making an illegal one.

"You're nuts. If you get caught, you could lose your license."

"I won't get caught. I just need to find someone who looks like me and is smart enough to pass the test."

By now we'd pulled in to Crazy Dave's Rent-A-Wreck, which indeed lived up to its name. The place was wall-to-wall clunkers. I almost expected to see Jed Clampett chugging along in his Model T.

"You can't possibly be serious about renting a car here," Kandi said, looking around, aghast.

"It's not so bad."

"Are you kidding? It looks like the aftermath of a demolition derby. C'mon, I'll take you to Hertz. My treat."

"I'll be fine," I said, with a confidence I didn't feel. "I'm sure these cars are perfectly safe."

I got out of the car and shooed her away.

"Go on, Kandi. I'm okay."

She shook her head, exasperated, and drove off, doing some heavy-duty tsk-tsking.

Once she was gone, I headed for a small office at the rear of the lot, where I found a bald butterball of a guy working at a computer, eating a piece of baklava. His scalp shone like a snow dome under the glare of the fluorescent lights.

A matching butterball woman, practically his twin, sat at a desk next to his, poring over account books with a chewed-up pencil.

"Er . . . Crazy Dave?" I said tentatively.

"That's me," the man boomed, in a thick Russian accent. "What can I do for you, lady?"

I told him I needed to rent a car for fifteen dollars a day, and much to my relief, he did not break out into gales of derisive laughter. On the contrary, he assured me he had the perfect car for me.

"Don't worry, lady," he said. "Crazy Dave will take good care of you."

I had a hunch his name wasn't really Dave. Mainly because the butterball lady kept pointing to his baklava and shrieking, "Watch out, Vladimir! Crumbs in the keyboard! Crumbs in the keyboard!"

Crazy Dave aka Vladimir led me outside. The place bore an uncanny resemblance to a parking lot in downtown Kabul. Not that I've ever actually been to downtown Kabul. I'm just guessing.

After looking at the wrecks—I mean, previously owned vehicles—in my price range, I finally settled on a decrepit VW Beetle so old I almost expected it to have a "Hitler for Führer" bumper sticker.

It was a stick shift and it had been years since I'd driven a shift, but I figured it would all come rushing back to me in no time. True, the car was painted a bilious green, and the fenders looked like they'd just lost a battle with an angry SUV. But Crazy Dave assured me my little VW would purr like a kitten.

Yeah, right. A kitten with asthma. Huge plumes of exhaust billowed out from the car the minute I turned on the ignition.

The less said about the ride home, the better. Sad to say, the art of driving a shift did not come rushing back to me. I popped the clutch and ground the gears the whole way home, bucking and lurching like a drunk on a mechanical bull.

When I finally shuddered to a stop in front of my apartment, I discovered that the locks were broken. Oh, well. Not a problem.

Nobody in their right mind was going to steal this clunker.

Chapter 4

"**P**rozac!" I wailed as I walked in the front door. "A horrible man stole my Corolla and stuck me with a lunch bill for two steak sandwiches and a tiramisu."

Her eyes wide with concern, the little darling leapt off the pile of freshly washed laundry she'd been napping on and came bounding to my side, rubbing my ankles in that comforting way she has when I'm down in the dumps.

Okay, she didn't move a muscle. She just yawned a yawn the size of the Grand Canyon and shot me a look that said, *Steak sandwiches, eh? Any leftovers?*

What can I say? Lassie, she's not.

I would've killed for a glass of chardonnay and/or a box of Oreos to calm my frazzled nerves, but I showed remarkable restraint and got down to the business at hand. (Mainly because I was all out of chardonnay and Oreos.)

I simply had to line up a job. I called my steady clients, but nobody had any work for me. I called my former clients (even the crazymakers I'd vowed I'd never work for again) and suffered through a series of dispiriting rejections. When my ear was numb from all those phone calls, I answered some on-line ads for jobs I knew I'd never get.

Exhausted, I plopped down on the sofa, trying to think of what else I could do. And then I remembered the nutcase who'd called me earlier that morning. The pantyhose-tossing comic. The last thing I wanted to do was write jokes for a woman whose punch line was a pair of underwear, but I had no choice. I was a desperado. I retrieved her number from my answering machine, then took a deep breath and made the call.

She picked up on the first ring. Why did I get the feeling this was a woman hovering over her phone, happy to hear from anyone, even a telemarketer?

"Dorcas MacKenzie," an eager voice came on the line. "Funnywoman Extraordinaire."

Not exactly Little Miss Modesty, was she?

"Hi," I said, trying to inject some enthusiasm into my voice. "This is Jaine Austen, returning your call."

"Oh, right! I'm so glad you called. Like I said on my message, I have an absolutely hysterical comedy act; it just needs to be tweaked here and there. Have you had any experience writing comedy?"

"Yes. In fact, I've had some sitcom experience."

Which was no lie. Some time back, I'd written a script for a sitcom that unfortunately never saw the light of day, due to a murder that took place during the taping of my show. It was a thrill-packed chapter in my life that should have taught me that working in show biz can be dangerous to your health.

"Really?" Dorcas sounded impressed. "You're a sitcom writer? What shows did you write for?"

"Only one show," I admitted. "*Muffy 'N Me.*"

"Oh." Now she sounded a lot less impressed. "I never heard of that one."

Okay, so it wasn't exactly *Seinfeld*, but then again, neither was she.

"I was hoping for someone with a bit more experience," she said, "but I'm willing to give it a shot if you are."

I cleared my throat and broached the subject at the fore-front of my mind.

"About salary . . ."

"Like I said on my message, I can't afford much. What would you say to five dollars a joke?"

I'd say something not suitable for a family novel, that's what I'd say.

"Dorcas, I couldn't possibly work for that amount."

"Six bucks?"

"My going rate is fifty dollars an hour."

I could hear her gasp on the other end of the line. "I can't afford fifty dollars an hour."

"How about forty?"

"How about we compromise and say ten?"

Ten dollars an hour? Was she kidding? That was barely above minimum wage. After all, I was a writer, a wordsmith. The woman who came up with *In a Rush to Flush? Call Toiletmasters!* Did she really think I'd sell my services for a measly ten dollars an hour?

Bridling with righteous indignation, I said the only thing possible under the circumstances: "Sure."

Hey, don't go shaking your head like that. What else could I do? It was ten dollars an hour more than I'd make sitting home on my fanny.

We agreed to meet for coffee at Pinky's Deli in West Holly-wood and I set off for the meeting, with a quick pit stop at the market for a bottle of chardonnay and some Oreos.

Something told me I'd be needing them.

An hour later, I came lurching up to Pinky's in my ancient VW, which I was now calling Wheezy. The drive over had been only slightly less harrowing than my maiden voyage. I was beginning to get the hang of driving a stick shift again, but poor Wheezy's asthma showed no signs of letting up. I managed to coax her into the parking lot and shut off the ignition with a sigh of relief.

Pinky's was a nondescript deli, with cracked vinyl booths and linoleum on the floor, a hangout for the comedians who performed at the Laff Palace across the street. It was four in the afternoon when I headed inside, and the place was nearly deserted.

A dark-haired woman sat in a booth at the front of the restaurant. I figured it had to be Dorcas. The only other customers in the restaurant were two guys in their eighties crumbling saltines into their chicken noodle soup.

I waved tentatively and walked over to join her.

The first thing I noticed about Dorcas was how skinny she was. Tall and gangly, and thin as a rail. Think Ichabod Crane with a ponytail.

It was hard to see much of her face. Most of it was obscured by the huge double-decker pastrami sandwich she was gulping down. It looked like the sandwich weighed more than she did.

"Hi," I said to the face behind the sandwich. "Are you Dorcas?"

She jumped up and nodded, her mouth filled with pastrami.

"You must be Jaine," she said, finally managing to swallow. She offered me a mustard-stained hand to shake and grinned a wide generous smile. "Grab a seat."

I slid into the booth across from her, wondering if she'd mind if I plucked a piece of pastrami dangling from her sandwich.

"You hungry?" she asked, following my gaze. "Want a pastrami sandwich? They make really good ones here."

"Oh, no. No, thanks."

There was no way I was going to order a pastrami sandwich—not after that huge lunch I'd had. Absolutely not.

"Hey, Mitzi," she shouted to a blowsy waitress whose jet black hair was tortured into a towering beehive. "Bring my friend here a pastrami sandwich."

"Really," I protested, "I shouldn't."

Then I called out to the waitress: "With a side of potato salad."

What can I say? I can't take me anywhere.

"Have a pickle while you're waiting," Dorcas said.

I plucked a fat pickle from a bowl on the table and took a bite. It was lip-puckering heaven.

"Forgive me for stuffing my face," she said between bites, "but I'm starving."

As I watched her eat, I couldn't help feeling a tad disgruntled. It certainly didn't seem fair that people like Dorcas could stuff their faces with pastrami and never gain an ounce, while fat cells clung to my thighs like barnacles to a ship.

"So," she said, when she finally came up for air, "I suppose you want to hear all about my act."

Not really. What I really wanted was that pastrami sandwich, but I was here to make money, so I plastered a bright smile on my face and said, "Sure. Shoot."

"Well, I start out my act—"

But before she could tell me how she started her act, a muscular guy in tight black jeans and a T-shirt came sauntering over to our table. He had the kind of oily good looks popular in singles bars and Vegas casinos.

"How's it going, Dork?" he sneered. "Put any audiences to sleep lately?"

She bit into a pickle with an angry snap of her jaw.

"Up yours, Vic."

Then he turned to me, his sneer still firmly in place.

"Last time I saw the Dork's act, she stank so bad people were waiting in line—to get out."

"Where'd you get that gag?" Dorcas said. "The museum

of prehistoric jokes? I think Plato was using it on open-mike night at the Acropolis."

Just then a skinny guy in jeans and a corduroy jacket appeared at Mr. Nasty's side and grabbed him by the elbow.

"C'mon, Vic," the skinny guy said, his Adam's apple bobbing like a yo-yo. "Let's go."

He gave Dorcas an apologetic smile and tugged his obnoxious friend to a table at the back of the restaurant.

"Hey, Vic!" Dorcas shouted after them. "Time to bring your hair in for an oil change.

"What a jerk," she said, turning back to me.

"I couldn't agree more. Is he a comic, too?"

"He thinks he is. Frankly, I think his act stinks. I can't understand why he's getting booked at comedy clubs and I'm not."

She glanced down at her now-empty plate and mopped up a speck of mustard with her pickle.

"It helps that he has Hank, of course."

"Hank?"

"The guy who dragged him away. Hank is his writer. He's the funny one. He gives Vic all his best jokes, and Vic hogs the credit. Why Hank puts up with Vic, I'll never know. The guy is a total bottom-feeder." She turned and glanced at where he was sitting. "See the cigarette lighter on his table?"

I looked over and saw a silver cigarette lighter at Vic's side.

"It's not really a lighter; it's a tape recorder. He uses it to steal other comics' jokes."

I gasped in disbelief. Not at Vic's thievery. But at the sight of our waitress approaching with a pastrami sandwich as big as a Chihuahua. I absolutely could not allow myself to finish it, not if I expected to have an unclogged artery left in my body.

Dorcas stared at it longingly.

I couldn't believe she was still hungry. Where the heck was she packing all those calories?

"You want half?" I asked, after the waitress had gone.

"Thanks," she said, sweeping it off my plate with the speed of a Hoover. I felt a twinge of annoyance. Yes, I know I just said I didn't want to finish the darn thing, but now that it was gone, I missed it.

I took a big bite of my half before she changed her mind and decided she wanted it, too. It was salty, greasy, and oozing with mustard. In other words, divine.

We spent the next minute or so with our mouths full of pastrami, so talk was pretty much out of the question. Over at Vic's table, I saw Vic flirting with Mitzi, the bouffant-haired waitress. The woman was twice his age and giggling like a teenager.

"He flirts with anything in a skirt," Dorcas said, following my gaze. "And the pathetic thing is, he's got a really nice girlfriend. Cheats on her right and left, and she hasn't a clue."

Dorcas had finished her half of the sandwich.

I clutched what was left of mine protectively. She'd have to wrestle me to the ground before I'd let her have it.

Accepting the fact that there was nothing left to eat except her place mat, Dorcas rolled up her paper napkin in a ball and tossed it on her plate. Then she reached into her purse and took out a beautiful cloisonné lipstick case. When she opened the case, I was surprised to see a tube of Chapstick nestled inside.

"You keep Chapstick in a beautiful case like that?" I asked.

"Oh, I never wear lipstick. It's a sexist symbol of feminine subjugation. A tool of the male-dominated media."

Huh? Was she talking about the same stuff I slapped on my lips to keep me from looking like a walking zombie?

"I love the case, though," she said, admiring the beautiful cloisonné design. "I bought it years ago, back when I was still trying to please men."

Hmmm. It looked like somebody at the table was channeling Betty Friedan through Germaine Greer.

"So," I said, figuring I might as well get it over with, "tell me about your act."

"It's a whole new kind of comedy. I tell jokes from a feminist sociological perspective."

Uh-oh. Not exactly an area ripe with chuckles.

Dorcas began an impassioned rant about how women were oppressed in a male-dominated society, how they were made to loathe their bodies by the media and forced to sacrifice their integrity and comfort for an unattainable ideal of beauty.

Her eyes shone with excitement, her hands waved wildly. The woman was a bundle of nervous energy. Maybe that's why she was able to pack away so much food and never gain a pound.

"And when I rip up my pantyhose and throw the pieces to the audience at the end of my act," she said, flinging her arms in the air, "it symbolizes my breaking the yoke of centuries of male oppression!"

Good heavens. It sounded more like an article in *Ms. Magazine* than a comedy routine. Not that I didn't agree with a lot of what she said, but there wasn't a laugh in sight.

"It's brilliant, isn't it?"

I nodded numbly.

"All it needs is a few jokes to spice it up. Think you can do it?"

Was she kidding? There was no way on earth I could make this stuff funny. Chris Rock, Ellen DeGeneres, and the writing staff of *The Simpsons* couldn't make this stuff funny. And I was just about to tell her so when I remembered a little thing called a "car" I was going to have to buy.

"Sure," I said, forcing the words out of my mouth. "I can do it."

"Great!"

We set up a date for me to see her act the next night at the Laff Palace.

"I just know that with you by my side," she said, "I'm going to be utterly hilarious."

As it turns out, with me by her side, she was going to be utterly screwed. And I wasn't exactly in for a day at Disneyland myself. If I'd known then what was coming down the pike, I would've taken the pastrami and run.

I was sprawled on my bed, sipping chardonnay and licking the filling out of Oreos, thinking about how my day had gone from hopeful to horrible in the blink of an eye. It had started out so promising, with the sun shining and the birds tweeting and a high-paying job in the offing. And then, before I knew what hit me, I was minus a car and stuck with a minimum-wage job writing jokes for the unfunniest woman on the planet.

I gazed down at Prozac, who was snoring on my chest, blasting me with fish fumes.

No doubt about it. Life—much like Prozac's breath—stunk.

At that moment, just when I was convinced that I was living under my own personal storm cloud, the phone rang. I let the machine get it.

"Jaine? It's Andrew Ferguson calling."

And just like that, my world was flooded with sunshine again.

You remember Andrew, don't you? You would if you'd read my last book (*The PMS Murder*, now available in paperback at all the usual places).

Andrew Ferguson was a world-class dollburger, a bank executive I'd met on a job interview. The minute I saw him, with his lanky build and sandy brown hair that curled sexily at the nape of his neck, I felt my napping hormones spring into action.

At the time, I didn't think I stood a ghost of a chance with him. Andrew was unquestionably adorable in a corporate Brooks Brothers kind of way. And I don't usually attract the Brooks Brothers type. (Shnooks Brothers is more my speed.)

Much to my utter amazement, he'd asked me out. But before we got a chance to get together, he was transferred a quatrillion miles away to Stuttgart, Germany. I was certain I'd heard the last of him. And now here he was. Back in my life!

I snatched up the phone, my heart racing.

"Andrew!"

"Hey, Jaine. How are you?"

"Um, fine," I said, wowing him with my witty repartee. "How are things in Germany?"

"Actually, I wouldn't know. I'm here in L.A."

He was here in L.A.! I forced myself to take a deep breath and calm down. I had to play it cool.

"Oh, my gosh!" I squealed. "That's fantastic!"

That was playing it cool, all right. Any cooler and he'd be scraping me off the ceiling.

"Anyhow," he said, "I was wondering if you'd like to get together."

For all eternity, if possible.

"I'd love to."

"How about lunch tomorrow?"

Lunch? I felt a momentary twinge of disappointment. I was hoping for something a bit more romantic. Like a candle-lit dinner with wine and soft music and an all-you-can-eat dessert bar. But what the heck? Maybe he didn't want to rush things. Hadn't I read a million times that the most enduring relationships start off slow?

"Sure," I stammered. "Lunch would be fine."

"Would you mind meeting me downtown?" he asked.

"I'm in the middle of a crazy project at the bank, and I can't take much time off."

"No problem."

He named a trendy downtown restaurant and we agreed to meet there at noon.

"Oh, Prozac!" I screeched the minute I hung up. "It was Andrew Ferguson! My potential significant other."

I scooped her up in my arms and did a little happy dance.

She peered at me through slitted eyes.

Wait a minute. I thought I was your significant other. Moi!

"Prozac, honey, you know I adore you, but I was hoping some day to connect with someone of my own species."

She squirmed out of my arms and gave me a reproachful look.

Have you forgotten about your history with men?

She had me there. The men in my life have been unquestionable duds, a series of losers who'd make cupid consider a career in accounting.

Take my first and only husband, The Blob. A charming guy who clipped his toenails in the kitchen sink and watched ESPN during sex. After four years of marriage to The Blob, I thought I'd sworn off men forever, but then Andrew came along, and I decided to give the hairy half of the population another chance.

"Oh, Prozac. Don't you see? Andrew's different from all the others."

She shot me a skeptical look.

Just don't come crying to me when you get your heart broken.

Then she jumped off the bed and, tail held high, stalked off to the living room.

I'll be sleeping on the sofa tonight.

"Oh, don't be that way."

I tried luring her back to bed with kitty treats and belly rubs, but she wouldn't budge.

Normally I can't sleep without her warm body purring next to mine, but that night was different. That night I drifted off to a deep sleep filled with delicious dreams of me and Andrew and an all-you-can-eat dessert bar.

YOU'VE GOT MAIL!

To: Jausten
From: Shoptillyoudrop
Subject: Good News

Hi, darling—

Keep your eye out for the UPS man. I sent you the most adorable Georgie O. Armany shorts set from the shopping channel, just $39.99 plus shipping and handling. It's got sequined palm trees all over it, perfect to wear on a date in L.A. (Hint, hint.) I do hope you're going out, sweetheart, and not sitting home with Paxil, who's a precious kitty but not exactly the son-in-law of my dreams.

Good news here in Florida. Daddy's six-month suspension from the Tampa Vistas clubhouse will be up next week.

Remember how they kicked him out for starting a food fight at Sunday brunch? He claimed he never threw that Belgian waffle at Ed Peters, that it just slipped off his plate, but I don't see how a waffle can "slip" three feet in the air clear across a table. And everybody knew Daddy was mad at Ed for beating him at miniature golf. It's true that Ed was gloating about it all through brunch and I guess Daddy just lost it and threw his waffle at him. And then Ed threw his popover back at Daddy. Which just escalated the whole thing until Daddy wound up hurling that deviled egg. If only it hadn't landed down Mrs. Stuyvesant's cleavage! She was one of our nicest social directors ever. She handed in her resignation the very next day, saying she couldn't put up with Daddy anymore.

I didn't blame the board of directors when they suspended Daddy for six months. Of course, I think they also should have suspended Ed Peters. But the board said that the food fight was Ed's first offense, and Daddy had a list of infractions a mile long.

Oh, well. It's all going to be over soon, thank heavens! All Daddy has to do is sign a contract promising to behave himself and his membership will be reinstated.

I've felt so guilty about leaving Daddy home alone these last six months I've hardly gone to the clubhouse at all. Both of us have been stuck home trying to make the best of things. Somehow Bingo's not as much fun when you're playing with only two people. Anyhow, I can't wait to get back in the swing of things.

That's about it for now, honey. Keep your eye out for the UPS man!

Love and kisses from,
Mom

P.S. More good news: I finally got around to cleaning out Daddy's closet and took two whole shopping bags of his ratty old clothes to the thrift shop!

To: Jausten
From: DaddyO
Subject: Betrayed!

Dear Lambchop—

You won't believe what your mother did. Without even consulting me, she gave away my priceless vintage clothing! All of it perfectly wearable. Just because something has a stain and maybe a few holes doesn't mean it's no good anymore.

What's especially galling is that she gave away my lucky Hawaiian shirt. The one with the bright orange hibiscuses on it. That shirt has brought me good luck for the past twenty years. Why, that's the shirt I was wearing when I saw Meryl Streep at the car wash. And when I found a practically new pair of sneakers in the Blockbusters parking lot. And when I guessed how many gumballs were in the jar at the Hop Li Chinese Barbeque Café and won free egg rolls for two!

If your mom thinks she's going to get away with this, she's crazy. I'm going to march her down to the thrift shop right now and make her get my clothes back—before some discerning buyer snaps them up.

Your betrayed,
Daddy

To: Jausten
From: Shoptillyoudrop
Subject: Hit the Roof

Daddy just about hit the roof when he found out I gave away his old clothes. The way he's been carrying on, you'd think I'd lost our life savings. He insists on dragging me down *to the thrift shop* to buy those silly rags back.

Oh, dear. I've got to run. He's out in the car, honking the horn.

More later,
Mom

P.S. I don't care what Daddy says. He never saw Meryl Streep at the car wash. Not unless Meryl drives a beat-up pickup truck with a bumper sticker that says: *Beer. It's Not Just for Breakfast Anymore.*

To: Jausten
From: Shoptillyoudrop
Subject: Humiliation!

Well, we're back from the thrift shop and all I can say is I've never been so embarrassed in all my life. Daddy barged in, shouting, "My wife stole my clothes!" I was so humiliated I wanted to hide behind the used armoires.

The thrift shop ladies were only too happy to give him his awful rags back. I'm surprised they accepted them in the first place.

Finally, we were all set to go when Daddy realized he was missing his "lucky" Hawaiian shirt, that orange monstrosity with gravy stains from the Eisenhower administration. He calls it a "classic." If by classic he means something that will look ridiculous year after year, I suppose he's right.

It's hard to believe, but someone actually bought the darn thing! When Daddy found out, he went ballistic. He insisted that they give him the name and address of the buyer. The ladies tried to tell him they don't keep those kind of records, but Daddy didn't believe them. He even suggested that one of them might have kept the shirt for herself. Did you ever hear of anything so ridiculous? Why would one of those sweet thrift shop ladies want his silly Hawaiian shirt?

He stormed out of the store, threatening to report them to the Better Business Bureau! After all Daddy put those poor ladies through, I didn't want to leave the store without buying anything. So I wound up getting an oil painting of dogs playing poker. It's a very cute painting but we simply don't have any room for it. I think I'll send it to you, darling. I'm sure it'll look lovely in your living room.

Much love from,
Mom

To: Jausten
From: DaddyO
Subject: Jinxed!

Dearest Lambchop,

I may never forgive your mother. Because of her, my lucky shirt is gone forever. Without it, I'm in big trouble. I can feel it in my bones. Bad things are going to happen.

Your jinxed,
Daddy

To: Jausten
From: Shoptillyoudrop
Subject: Jinxed?

Daddy's convinced that without his lucky shirt he's jinxed. Did you ever hear of anything so silly?

Wait a minute. Now he's shouting about something. I'll be right back. . . .

Oh, dear. You won't believe what just happened. Daddy's computer crashed! You don't suppose he's right about being jinxed, do you?

Chapter 5

Prozac was still in a snit the next morning, wriggling out of reach when I tried to give her her morning back massage. The minute she finished inhaling her breakfast, she leapt up on top of my bookcase, as far away from me as possible.

Yes, she was in major prima donna mode, but I didn't care. All I could think about was my lunch date with Andrew. I'd forgotten all about yesterday's disastrous events and was floating around the apartment on a cloud of unrealistic expectations. By the time I'd nuked my morning coffee, I was mentally ordering flowers for our wedding.

Nothing could bring me down off my Andrew high. Not even those ominous e-mails from my parents.

I smelled trouble ahead. When it comes to Daddy, there's always trouble ahead. Daddy attracts trouble like white cashmere attracts wine stains. Not that I believed he was actually "jinxed." The only person jinxed in that relationship was Mom.

True, Mom could never remember Prozac's name and was constantly bombarding me with unwanted gifts. But she's a darling woman. And now Daddy would drive her crazy for weeks, if not months to come, over his "lucky" Hawaiian shirt.

But for once, I wasn't bothered by the scent of impending

disaster. Nor was I troubled by the prospect of a sequined shorts set and dogs playing poker showing up at my doorstep.

Que sera, sera. That was my motto du jour.

After checking my e-mails, I took a deliciously long bath, up to my neck in strawberry-scented bubbles. By the time I got out, Andrew and I had just bought our first house in the suburbs.

Then I blow-dried my curly mop till it was smooth as silk and floated into the bedroom to get dressed for my date. I tried on several outfits before going with jeans, an Ann Taylor blazer, and a fabulous pair of high-heeled suede boots I'd bought on sale at Bloomie's.

I surveyed myself in the mirror and saw, to my delight, that yesterday's monstrous zit was barely noticeable. After a dab of make-up and a spritz of hair spray, I was ready to go.

Out in the living room, Prozac was still perched on top of my bookcase.

"Bye, darling!" I called out to her as I headed for the door. "You still mad at me?"

She glared at me through slitted eyes and began clawing the paint off my bookcase.

I took that as a yes.

I was heading down the path to my car when I saw my neighbor Lance stretched out in a lounge chair outside his apartment. Lance and I share a quaint 1940s duplex on the fringes of Beverly Hills, where the rents are manageable and the plumbing is impossible.

Lance works flexible hours as a shoe salesman at Neiman Marcus, which gives him plenty of time to loll about on lounge chairs in the middle of the day. That morning he was wearing cut-off jeans and nothing on top, not an ounce of flab visible on his perfect bod.

"Hey, Jaine." He looked me up and down and nodded approvingly. "Nice outfit."

I beamed. That was high praise indeed from a guy who says moths come to my closet to commit suicide.

"Thanks!" I preened.

Then his eyes narrowed suspiciously.

"Those jeans don't have an elastic waist, do they?"

Lance hates elastic-waist pants. He thinks they're classless and tacky and very Jerry Springer. I keep telling him that they're comfortable, and he keeps telling me that I've got to suffer for beauty. Yeah, right. The only thing I'm willing to suffer for is a hot fudge sundae.

"No," I assured him, "they're not elastic waist."

To prove it, I opened my blazer and showed him the uncomfortable set-in waistband.

"Whatever you do," he warned, "don't unbutton the waistband. We don't want to look like a lady teamster, do we?"

"I won't unbutton the waistband."

"You promise?"

"I swear on a stack of J.Crew catalogs."

He smiled, satisfied.

"So where are you off to?"

"Oh, just a lunch date," I said, playing it nonchalant.

"Date?" He sat up, interested. "Did I hear the word *date* coming from your lips?"

I nodded.

"It's about time! I was beginning to think you were a nun."

"It's not that bad," I protested.

"Honey, the last time you were out, they were dancing the minuet."

"Harty-har."

"So who's the lucky guy?"

"A bank executive. I met him on a job interview last year."

"Cute?"

"Adorable."

"Well, if it doesn't work out, give him my number."

"Will do."

He beamed an encouraging smile.

"You look terrific, Jaine. Really."

With Lance's approval ringing in my ears, I headed down the path to Wheezy, where I unbuttoned the waistband on my jeans and set off for my date with Andrew.

I debated about whether or not to take the freeway. I doubted Wheezy could dredge up the energy to go more than forty miles an hour. But cross-town street traffic would be a nightmare, so I decided to risk it.

And so I spent the next twenty harrowing minutes clutching the wheel with white knuckles as Wheezy coughed and sputtered her way in the slow lane. Pedestrians were making better time than I was.

I'm happy to report that Wheezy didn't conk out on the freeway. Nope, she conked out 60 seconds after we got off the freeway. I was stopped at a traffic light when I looked down and saw all the warning lights blinking merrily on the dashboard.

I tried gunning the engine. Nothing. Poor Wheezy had breathed her last breath.

I checked my watch. It was five of noon, and I was at least fifteen blocks away from The Patio, the restaurant where I was supposed to meet Andrew. No way was I going to make it there in five minutes. Not in my fashionably high-heeled boots.

Suddenly I heard a blast of car horns. I turned and saw a line of cars backed up behind me. I motioned them to go around me.

I was sitting there, blocking traffic and cursing Crazy Dave and his wreckmobiles, when I heard someone tapping on my car window. I looked up and saw a tall black man. His name was Leonard. At least that was the name embroidered on his denim work shirt.

"Can I help you, lady?" he asked when I rolled down the window.

I looked up into his eyes. They were kind eyes, warm and sympathetic.

And then out of the blue, before I could stop myself, I was crying. With big hiccupy racking sobs.

This is crazy, I told myself. What was I doing crying in front of a perfect stranger? And ruining my eye make-up, too. But I couldn't stop myself.

"Lady, what's wrong?"

"Oh, Leonard!" I wailed. "First my car was stolen and then my insurance company gave me fifteen crummy dollars a day to rent a car and I got stuck with this lousy piece of junk and I finally got a date with the man of my dreams and he asked me to meet him for lunch and I crawled along the freeway with my knuckles practically welded to the steering wheel, and just when everything was looking okay Wheezy died."

Leonard shook his head sadly.

"I'm so sorry for your loss."

"My loss?"

"The deceased. This Weezie person."

"Oh, Wheezy's not a person. It's my car."

"I see," he said, nodding much like I imagine orderlies nod to out-of-control mental patients before they strap them into straightjackets. I fully expected him to back away and beat a hasty retreat, but instead, he took out an impeccably clean hanky from his pocket and handed it to me.

"Blow your nose," he said gently. "Everything's going to be fine. I'll get you to that lunch of yours."

What an angel. I made up my mind then and there that if I ever had a child, I was going to name it Leonard. Provided it was a boy, of course.

"But first," he said, "let's get this car of yours out of traffic."

He had me put the car in neutral and steer it while he pushed it to the curb.

"You can call a tow truck when you're ready to go home," he said when we were through. "Now let's head over to my van, and I'll give you a lift."

Was he the nicest guy in the world, or what? Hope began to seep back into my heart. Maybe this day wouldn't be a total washout after all.

Then I saw his van and gulped. Leonard, it turned out, was an exterminator. For a company called Bug Blasters. And the van he drove had a 6-foot replica of a dead bug, straight out of Kafka, lying belly up on top of it.

Oh, well, I told myself. So it wasn't a limo. Big deal. Beggars can't be choosers.

"Hop inside," he said, sliding the door open.

And then suddenly I got scared. Leonard seemed like a wonderful guy, the very definition of a Good Samaritan, but hey, so did Ted Bundy. And I hear Jack the Ripper was a lot of laughs at parties. What if Leonard was a secret sex fiend planning to have his way with me under the giant bug?

I could practically hear my mother shouting: *Never get into cars with strangers!*

But then I thought of Andrew and the way his hair curled at the nape of his neck, and threw caution to the wind.

I hopped on board.

It turned out that Leonard was as nice as could be, an absolute doll, who gave me all sorts of handy tips about getting rid of ants. (Boric acid along your baseboards works wonders, in case you're interested.) We zipped over to The Patio in no time.

"Here we are," he said, pulling up in front of the restaurant. "Only ten minutes late."

"Oh, Leonard. How can I ever thank you?"

"Let me give you my card, in case you ever need an exterminator."

I took his card and promised to call him at the first signs of termites, cockroaches, earwigs, and/or silverfish.

Then I turned to open the van door and gulped in dismay.

I'd never been to The Patio before, and I now saw that the restaurant took its name from a spacious outdoor patio facing the street. A patio which was, at that moment, filled to capacity with upscale, well-groomed diners—all of whom were gawking at the van with the giant dead bug on top.

Dear Lord, I prayed. *Please don't let Andrew be sitting outside.*

But there he was, out on The Patio's patio, gawking at the van like everybody else.

Oh, crud. What would he think of me, showing up for our date in a Bug Blasters' van? I considered telling Leonard to drive to the next block and that I'd walk back, but he'd been so nice to me I couldn't insult him by letting him see that I was ashamed of his profession.

There was no getting out of it. I gritted my teeth and climbed down out of the van, treating the al fresco diners to a swell view of my tush.

It was a toss-up over which of us looked more ridiculous: me or the dead bug.

Gathering what was left of my dignity, I made my way to Andrew's table, trying to ignore the stares following in my wake.

Andrew stood up to greet me, looking yummy in a pin-stripe suit, his hair curling seductively over his collar, just as I remembered it.

"That was quite an entrance," he said, barely suppressing a smile. "Did you know your butt looks really big climbing out of an exterminator's van?"

Okay, he didn't really say the part about my butt. I just prayed he wasn't thinking it.

I plopped down in my chair and explained what happened to Wheezy.

"What rotten luck," he said when I was through. "But don't worry. We'll call a tow service after lunch and take care of everything."

He smiled a reassuring smile.

I just love men with reassuring smiles, don't you?

"Anyhow," he said, "I hope you like this restaurant."

"Oh, I do."

"If not, there's a Roach Motel nearby."

Okay, he didn't say that, either. My imagination was in overdrive.

What he actually said was: "I'm sorry I dragged you all the way downtown, but I've been working night and day on a project. With Sam Weinstock. You remember Sam don't you?"

Inwardly I groaned. I remembered Sam, all right. Sam—short for Samantha—Weinstock was the CFO of Andrew's bank, a stunning woman with the face of a Clinique model and a waist the size of my ankle. When I'd met her last year, I was sure she and Andrew were a hot item.

Just the thought of her made me feel ten pounds heavier.

"Actually," Andrew said, "she's here in the restaurant, having lunch with a friend."

Drat. The last thing I wanted was to be in comparison range with the spectacular size two Sam.

"In fact, she's right over there."

I followed his gaze to where Sam was sitting across from another razor-thin bizgal. If I'd been harboring any secret hopes that working long hours had taken its toll on Sam, I was in for a disappointment. She was as spectacular as ever, her delicate face framed by a gleaming crown of chestnut hair, not a single one of which dared stray out of place.

Andrew waved to her, and the next thing I knew she was getting up and heading in our direction. I hoped against hope that she was going to the ladies room, but no such luck. She slithered straight to our table.

"Hello, Jaine," she said coolly.

"Hi," I managed to mutter.

I just prayed she hadn't seen me show up in the giant bug-mobile.

Once again, my prayers went unanswered.

"So good to see you again," she said, a malicious glint in her eyes. "What a colorful entrance you made."

"Yes, my Rolls is in the shop. Haha."

Andrew smiled at my feeble attempt at humor. Sam didn't.

"How've you been?" she asked. "Still writing toilet bowl ads?"

"As a matter of fact, I am," I said, wishing with all my heart I could flush her down a Big John.

"Well, don't be too long," she said to Andrew, wagging her finger at him playfully. "We've still got lots of work to do, hon."

Accent on the *hon*.

Then she waved good-bye, an irritating little flicker of her hand, and slithered back to her bizgal friend.

As I watched her walk across the room, resplendent in her size two suit, I felt every ounce of confidence drain from my body. I'd been a fool to think Andrew was interested in me. Anyone who'd dated a woman like Sam couldn't possibly be interested in me.

This wasn't a date, I realized. It was a business lunch. Andrew probably wanted to offer me a job writing brochures for the bank. My initial instincts had been right. If he were really interested in me, he'd have asked me out to a candlelit dinner.

"So," Andrew said, "you're still working for Toiletmasters."

What did I tell you? He was asking me about work. It had to be a business lunch.

"Yes, I'm still in the toilet. Haha. And how about you? You still at the bank? What am I saying? Of course you're still at the bank. Otherwise why would you be working on a project with Sam? Unless you were working in some other profession and freelancing as a banker. I suppose that's possible. Not likely, of course. But possible . . ."

Oh, Lord. I was babbling again. Damn that Sam. She'd totally thrown me for a loop. Before I could stop myself, I reached for a sourdough roll and smeared it with butter. Now Andrew was going to think I was a butter-slathering blabbermouth. Oh, well. Who cared? He wasn't interested in me anyway.

Thank heavens the waiter showed up to take our order and put an end to my inane chatter. Andrew and I both ordered the Patioburgers with fries.

"That's what I like about you," Andrew said when the waiter had gone. "You eat like a real person." He watched as I shoveled down my buttered roll. "So many women I've dated spend the entire meal pushing three shards of lettuce around their plate and then say they're stuffed. That's no fun."

"So," he said, taking a roll from the basket. "You seeing anybody?"

Whoa. I almost choked on my sourdough. Maybe this *was* a date after all.

"No, nobody on a regular basis."

If you don't count the Domino's delivery guy.

"Me neither," he said, smearing his roll with butter.

"What about Sam? I thought you two were dating."

"We were, but that's all over now."

I glanced over at Sam's table. Her lunch companion was chattering away a mile a minute, but Sam was staring past her and watching us with eagle eyes. Maybe Andrew thought it was all over, but it sure didn't look like Sam got the message.

"Anyhow," he said, "I've been wanting to ask you out. But . . ."

He stared down at his roll and hesitated.

But what? What's stopping you? Go ahead! Here I am! Ready and available!

". . . but I'm not sure it would be fair to you."

"Why wouldn't it be fair?"

"You see, I'm only going to be in L.A. for a short time, and then I've got to go back to Stuttgart."

"You're going back to Germany?" I said, not bothering to hide my disappointment.

"I'm afraid so. And while I'm here I'm barely going to have a minute to myself. This project Sam and I are working on is taking up practically all my time."

"I'll bet she is—I mean, I'll bet it is."

He took a bite of his roll. A tiny dot of butter clung to his cheek.

Only Andrew could look sexy with butter on his cheek.

"Having loaded you down with warnings," he said, "I'm hoping you'll still want to have dinner with me."

He shot me a heart-melting grin.

No, I told myself, absolutely not. Why start something that couldn't possibly go anywhere? I knew what would happen. We'd go out and I'd fall head over heels in love and he'd go off to Stuttgart and meet some blond fräulein and forget all about me. Prozac was right. I'd just wind up getting hurt. Scrumptious as he was, there was no way I was going out with this guy.

So I hardened my heart, looked him straight in the eye, and said, "Sure."

What can I say? Andrew was like a pint of Chunky Monkey in my freezer. Impossible to resist.

Our burgers came and I didn't bother to pretend I was a dainty eater. I dove into mine with gusto. Hadn't Andrew just said he liked a gal with a hearty appetite? I would've liked the opportunity to impress him with my dessert-eating skills, but there was no time for dessert. The instant our waiter whisked away our lunch dishes, Sam popped up at our table, reminding Andrew that they still had lots of work to do at the bank.

Andrew quickly paid the bill and drove me to Wheezy, where we phoned for a tow truck and sat back to wait.

There we were, just the two of us, as snug as two bugs in a BMW. I should've been in seventh heaven. But instead I was suddenly flooded with doubts. What was I doing with this guy, anyway? We were worlds apart. He was upper crust and I was pizza crust. Sure, he was cuter than cute, but what if, underneath that yummy exterior, he was Sam's counterpart, an elitist snob?

"How about a strawberry?" he said, interrupting my thoughts. He reached for a box of strawberries in the back-seat.

"Thanks," I said, plucking one from the box. "They look delicious."

"I bought 'em from one of those guys on the freeway."

In Los Angeles, there are always poor souls standing on freeway off-ramps selling flowers and fruit. I dread to think how little they're paid to stand in the blazing sun breathing in carcinogens all day. Most drivers just zoom past them, but every once in a while, some kind soul will stop and buy their wares.

It heartened me to think that Andrew was one of those souls.

"Aren't you going to have one?" I said when he didn't take any.

"No, I'm allergic to strawberries."

"You mean you bought the strawberries even though you can't eat them?"

He nodded. "The guy looked so sad I couldn't say no."

At that moment, any doubts I had about Andrew flew out the window. He was obviously the warmhearted softie of my dreams.

I wanted nothing more than to linger in the BMW with him, trading life stories and running my fingers through his curls. But that was not to be. Not three minutes after Andrew offered me that strawberry, the Triple A guy came roaring up and with lightning speed had Wheezy hooked up and ready to tow.

"I'll call you soon," Andrew said, beaming me a megawatt smile, "and we'll set up our dinner date."

I came *thisclose* to hurling myself across the stick shift and into his lap for a torrid good-bye kiss, but you'll be happy to know I restrained myself.

Instead, I hoisted myself into the cab of the tow truck (treating Andrew to another scenic view of my tush) and headed off to vent my spleen on Crazy Dave.

"One of my cars is broke? Impossible!"

Crazy Dave aka Vladimir polished off the piece of baklava he was eating and shook his bald head, incredulous.

"Crazy Dave's cars never break!"

Yeah, right. Crazy Dave probably had a place of honor in the Tow Truck Hall of Fame.

"Maybe you just need change of oil," he said.

"How about I keep the oil and change the car?"

"No! No!" he insisted. "Nothing wrong with car."

After wiping his sticky fingers on his jeans, he opened the engine hood and peered inside.

"Aha!" he exclaimed, with all the solemnity of Einstein discovering the Theory of Relativity. "I see problem! The fan belt snapped. Happens all the time. To fix is easy-sneezy, one two three!"

He went scurrying into his office and minutes later came out waving a dirty fan belt.

"Practically brand new," he exclaimed.

And true to his word, in no time at all he'd changed the fan belt. I got in the car, started the engine and Wheezy sputtered back to life.

"See?" Crazy Dave beamed. "Nothing wrong with car. Good as new!"

Wheezy belched a huge cloud of exhaust.

"Still purring like kitten," he said, stroking her hood.

"Right," I sighed, then started to pull out of the lot. I hadn't gone very far when I looked in my rearview mirror and saw Crazy Dave running after me, holding something in his hand.

"Wait!" he cried.

He caught up to the car, breathless.

"I have something for you."

He held out a gooey hunk of baklava wrapped in waxed paper.

"A present," he beamed, grinning. "To make up for your troubles."

I looked down at the baklava in his greasy hands. This was his idea of making amends? Well, if he thought he could buy me off with a measly piece of baklava—he was absolutely right. I scarfed it down at the first traffic light.

So much for venting my spleen.

Chapter 6

The last thing I wanted to do that night was see Dorcas's comedy act, but she was my one and only client, and so, after a nutritious dinner of peanut butter and pretzels, I got in Wheezy and headed over to the Laff Palace.

The club was on a busy street in the heart of West Hollywood, where parking spaces at night are as scarce as straight men.

I drove around searching for a spot for about ten minutes. Finally, I gave up and handed Wheezy over to the Laff Palace's valet parking guy, a skinny teenager in a red jacket and black bow tie.

He looked at the ancient VW in disdain.

"You want me to park it—or shoot it and put it out of its misery?"

Obviously, a budding comic.

I tried to think of a snappy comeback, but what could I tell him? That my real car was a Corolla? So I just tossed him the keys and headed inside.

If I could pick one word to describe the Laff Palace, it wouldn't be *palatial*. A dark, cavernous room with a tiny stage up front, it had all the charm of a meat locker. At eight o'clock, early in the evening in the comedy world, the place was only half full.

A bouncy barmaid in tight shorts and a T-shirt that said *Cute, but Psycho* came up to me, holding her round bar tray aloft. She wore her jet black hair in a ponytail at the top of her head, Pebbles-style.

"Table for one?" she asked.

"No," I told her, "I'm with Dorcas MacKenzie, one of the comics."

"Oh, her," she said dismissively. "She's over at the bar. She pointed a neon pink fingernail to a bar at the back of the room. Then she trotted off with her drinks, her ponytail swishing as she walked.

I headed over to a worm-eaten bar and inhaled the intoxicating aroma of beer and Lysol.

Dorcas sat at the end of the bar, sipping a Coke through a straw.

"Hi, Dorcas!" I said, with fake enthusiasm, as I sat down next to her. "How's it going?"

"Okay, I guess." She looked about as happy as a condemned prisoner waiting for her last meal to show up.

"Actually," she confessed, "I'm a little nervous. I always get nervous before I go on."

I'd be nervous, too, if I had an act like hers.

"I'm sure you'll be great," I lied.

At the other end of the bar, the nasty comic I'd seen at the deli was deep in conversation with his writer.

"Isn't that the guy I saw the other day at Pinky's?" I asked.

"Yeah, that's Slick Vic. All the comics hang out at the bar while we wait to go on."

Indeed, I saw a few other guys standing around, mumbling their monologues to themselves. Dorcas was the only woman in the bunch.

It was Open Mike night at the club, a night when they let anyone get up and perform. Apparently regardless of talent. Up onstage a chubby guy oozing flop sweat was trying in vain to amuse the audience by making fart noises with his under-arms.

"They always put the weak acts on first," Dorcas explained, "and save the stronger comics for later."

"Which means you should've been on hours ago," Vic quipped.

The comics at the bar snickered, and Dorcas turned red.

"Shove it up your kazoo, Vic," she shot back.

At which point, the bartender, a beefy guy who looked like he could moonlight as an extra on *The Sopranos*, came over to take my order.

"Hey, Pete," Dorcas said. "This is Jaine, my writer."

"Nice to meetcha," he said, with a wink.

I got the not very pleasant feeling that Pete was taking a shine to me.

"So you're gonna write for Dorcas, huh?"

"Lots of luck," Vic called out. "You're gonna need it."

"Just ignore him, Dorcas," Pete said, loud enough for Vic to hear. "He's a jerk."

I could see Vic's jaw clench in anger, but Pete was a refrigerator of a guy, and Vic was no dummy. He pretended not to hear.

"So what'll you have, sweetheart?" Pete said to me, wiping a glass with a dishcloth that looked like it had just come from a car wash.

I figured anything that didn't come in a glass was a safe choice.

"I'll have a bottled water."

"That'll be six bucks."

Six bucks for a crummy bottle of water?

"Plus a three-drink minimum."

There went my first week's salary.

"But for you," he said, with another wink, "I'll make it a two-drink minimum."

"Then I'll live it up and have two bottled waters."

Pete flashed me a gap-toothed grin and hurried off to get my waters.

At a nearby table, I saw a customer eating a burger and fries. The fries looked pretty darn good, and I was tempted to order them. But if the kitchen was as filthy as Pete's dishcloth, I didn't want to risk it.

"Is it safe to order the food here?" I asked Dorcas.

"Not unless you've got a stomach pump in your purse. Rumor has it the chef seasons his burgers with sweat."

"I guess I'll stick with water."

"Smart choice."

By now the fart comic had farted his last fart, and a pot-bellied emcee came bounding onstage. He wore an electric-blue jumpsuit unzipped halfway to his navel, exposing a small forest of chest hair, and enough gold chains to stock a QVC warehouse.

"Interesting fashion statement," I said.

"That's Spiro Papadalos," Dorcas said. "He owns the club."

For his sake, I hoped he had better taste in comics than he had in clothes.

Spiro proceeded to introduce a "hot new comic" making his "debut appearance" on the Laff Palace stage. A gangly guy in jeans, T-shirt, and a blazer, which seemed to be the standard stand-up outfit, came out onstage, terror shining in his eyes.

Something told me this was his debut appearance on any stage. He had no confidence whatsoever. He mumbled his material and was sweating into the mike so badly I was afraid he'd electrocute himself.

"Where'd Spiro dig up this guy?" Vic said loudly. "He makes Dorcas look like David Letterman."

The other comics laughed and Vic looked particularly proud of himself, having managed to trash two comics at once.

Just then I noticed a fragile beauty with long Botticelli hair approaching the bar with a violin case.

"That's Allison," Dorcas whispered, following my gaze. "Vic's girlfriend. She's a concert violinist. She must've just come from a rehearsal."

"She looks sweet," I said.

"She is. Way too sweet for a creep like Vic."

"Does she always bring her violin with her to the club?" I asked.

Dorcas nodded. "Last year her violin got stolen from her car, and now she won't let this one out of her sight. Especially not around here. It's not exactly the safest neighborhood."

That was encouraging news. Maybe someone would steal Wheezy and then Crazy Dave would be forced to give me another car.

Allison walked over to Vic and kissed him on the cheek.

"Hi, babe!" Vic called out, not bothering to lower his voice.

Vic's writer, Hank, smiled at Allison shyly, then quickly went back to making notes on index cards.

"So, babe," Vic boomed. "How'd the rehearsal go?"

"Shhh, honey," she said, glancing at the comic onstage. "You're talking too loud. The audience won't be able to hear him."

"Trust me," Vic said. "I'll be doing them a favor."

The audience burst out laughing. Much to Vic's chagrin, the gangly comic onstage had scored with a joke.

I looked up and saw he was looking a lot more sure of himself. The tide had turned. The audience, previously indifferent, had decided they liked him. And with good reason. Now that he'd stopped mumbling, he was a funny guy.

Dorcas poked me in the ribs.

"Watch Vic," she whispered. "I bet he takes out his recorder."

Sure enough, now that he realized the kid onstage was getting laughs, Vic took out his "cigarette lighter" and pressed a button.

I shook my head in amazement. This guy made pond scum look classy.

The comic finished his act to loud applause and Spiro came bounding onstage, gold chains flashing, thrilled at last to have someone getting laughs in the Laff Palace.

Spiro wasn't so lucky with his next act, the Incredible Roberto, a guy who told bad jokes while juggling steak knives. One false move, I thought, and he'd be the Incredible Roberta.

By now, I'd finished the first of my six-dollar waters and needed to take a tinkle. I excused myself and asked one of the barmaids for directions to the ladies' room. She pointed down a long dark corridor.

"Last door on the right."

I walked down the hall past a couple of doors till I got to the ladies' room, a disgusting cubicle that had last been disinfected when mastodons roamed the earth. I'll spare you the gory details. I'm only bringing up my trip to the ladies' room because of what happened when I was through.

I was heading back down the hallway, wishing I'd brought along a spray can of Lysol, when I heard a woman's voice raised in anger.

"I've had enough of your excuses!"

It was coming from one of the rooms along the corridor. The door was partially open, and I peeked inside.

What can I say? I'm nosy.

It was a supply room, and standing there among the crates of swizzle sticks and Brand X booze was Pebbles, the *Cute, but Psycho* barmaid, looking pissed. And the object of her hissy fit was none other than Vic.

"When are you going to tell Allison about us, Vic?"

"Soon, baby," he said, stroking her cheek. "Real soon."

"That's what you said six months ago," she said, swatting his hand away.

"Hey, it's not easy. Allison and I have been together for three years."

"I don't care how long you've been together. You promised me you'd leave her. And you'd better do it. Or you'll be sorry."

At that moment, her ponytail quivering with rage, she seemed to live up to the *Cute, but Psycho* warning plastered across her chest.

Then she turned on her heels and headed for the door.

Which was my cue to get the heck out of there.

"What took you so long?" Dorcas was a bundle of nerves when I got back to the bar. "I go on any minute."

She picked up an oversized tote bag from the floor and set it on the bar. I peeked inside and saw that it was filled to the brim with pantyhose.

"I buy them by the gross," she said, grabbing a pair and stuffing it into one of her pants pockets.

"So you don't actually take them off onstage," I said, relieved that she wasn't going to be doing a strip act.

"And perpetuate a perverted male sexual fantasy? No way!"

Then she reached into the tote and pulled out a pair of scissors, which she shoved into her other pocket. Finally, she took out her cloisonné lipstick case and slapped on some Chapstick.

"And now," Spiro was saying, "let's welcome to the Laff Palace stage a very funny lady, Dorcas MacKenzie."

"Bombs away!" Vic called out, setting off a fresh round of guffaws from the comics at the bar.

Dorcas flushed in dismay.

"Don't listen to them," I said, squeezing her arm. "You'll be great."

She put on a brave smile and hurried up to the stage. I admired her courage. It takes a lot of guts to be a comic, especially when you don't have any actual jokes.

Dorcas got up to the mike and started to do the same material I'd heard in the deli. It hadn't gotten any funnier since then. The same feminist diatribe about women being forced to conform to unrealistic ideals of beauty. All very true. All very boring.

The audience wasn't paying attention. People were ordering drinks and talking among themselves, biding their time until the next act came on.

And I'm ashamed to confess my mind did a little wandering of its own. I thought back to the scene I'd just witnessed in the darkened corridor. So Vic was cheating on his girlfriend with Pebbles the barmaid. I wasn't surprised. Hadn't Dorcas told me Vic flirted with anything in a skirt?

I looked across the bar at Allison, one of the few people in the audience not talking over Dorcas's act. I could see the pity in her eyes as she watched Dorcas dying up onstage. Allison was clearly a kind soul; what was she doing with a guy like Vic? He was probably one of those rats who, in spite of their rat-hood, manage to charm their way into the hearts—and panties—of good women. Sad to say, there's a lot of that going around.

For a fleeting instant, I wanted to run over and tell her what a creep he was and how he was cheating on her with Pebbles. But of course, I didn't.

Instead, I was jolted out of my reverie by angry booing coming from the audience. Somehow, in just minutes, the audience had turned from bored to hostile. Dorcas was ranting her feminist spiel to a roomful of mainly drunk jocks. And the natives were getting restless. They wanted someone on stage who'd tell the bathroom humor they were so fond of.

Finally, her act came to a merciful close. She cut up her

pantyhose with her scissors and threw the bits out into the audience.

The only laugh she got all night came next, when Vic shouted, "Forget the pantyhose, Dork, and throw out your act."

The audience roared.

Poor Dorcas came back to the bar, her face burning with humiliation.

"Hey, Dork," Vic sneered. "Want a little constructive criticism? You stink."

His toadies at the bar snickered.

"Screw you, Vic," Dorcas said. Then she took a big gulp of her Coke and muttered, "I'd like to kill that bastard."

"I'd like to help," I said.

And I meant every syllable.

Now if I'd just bombed the way Dorcas bombed, I wouldn't dream of hanging around the scene of my humiliation. I'd hightail it out of there back home to my bathtub so fast your head would spin. But not Dorcas. She plunked herself down at the bar and ordered a double scotch from Pete the bartender.

"Anything for you, sweetheart?" Pete asked me.

"No," I said, holding up my six-dollar water bottle. "I'm fine."

"I guess Vic's right," Dorcas said, with a sigh. "I stink."

"That's not true," I lied. "You have some very funny material. Like you said, it just needs tweaking."

She looked up from where she was tearing a cocktail napkin to shreds.

"You really think so?"

No! I wanted to scream. *Of course I don't think so. You're about as funny as an open wound. You're never going to make it, so quit now and save yourself the heartache.*

But she was looking at me with such hope in her eyes I couldn't bear to bust her bubble.

"Sure," I managed to say.

"Hey, I've got an idea," she said, brightening. "Let's stay here and work on my act."

"Here? Don't you think it's a little too noisy?"

"Nah," she said, with a wave of her swizzle stick. "It'll be fine."

I had absolutely no idea what to do with her act, other than burn it, but it didn't matter, because Dorcas didn't really want to work that night. What Dorcas really wanted was to get drunk. Which she did, with impressive speed.

By the time she'd finished her second scotch, all her confidence had come bouncing back, and she was convinced that the people in the audience were a bunch of lowlife boors who wouldn't appreciate true comedy if it sat on their lap.

I spent the next forty-five minutes listening to Dorcas trash the audience and nursing my six-dollar water. I'd be damned if I'd spend one more cent in this place, although by now the smell of those fries was driving me crazy.

Meanwhile a series of foulmouthed comics took their turn onstage doing acts that would make a longshoreman blush. The jocks in the audience ate it up. I like comedy as much as the next person (provided the next person isn't the Marquis de Sade), but I just didn't get it. What the heck was so funny about the F word? The only time I ever found the F word remotely laughable was when I was doing it with The Blob.

No, my idea of a funny four-letter word was *Lucy*.

But nobody was asking me my idea, and the locker room language was getting solid laughs.

By now, the place had filled up. Most all the tables were taken when Vic was finally called up onstage.

"Ladies and gentlemen," Spiro was saying, "let's give a

warm Laff Palace welcome to a rising young comic star, Vic Cleveland!"

More than anything, I wanted Vic to bomb. But in the Life Isn't Fair department, he was very funny. He had strong jokes and terrific timing. And amazingly enough, once onstage he actually seemed likeable. Gone was the smarmy comic shooting zingers. Under the spotlight, Vic was an affable guy with a disarming grin. Even when he started taking some cheap shots at his ex-wife, he was still funny. The audience loved him.

I was sitting there musing on the injustice of it all when I felt someone poke me in the ribs.

I turned to see a rumpled man in his sixties on the bar stool next to mine. His sports jacket had clearly seen better days, and his few remaining hairs were plastered across his head in a hideous comb-over.

"That's my client!" he said, his barrel chest puffing with pride. I was guessing he'd once been a muscular guy, but those muscles had long ago turned to flab.

"I'm Vic's agent. Manny Vernon." He fished out a business card from his pocket and handed it to me. "Of The Manny Vernon Agency."

The card was dog-eared at the edges and blotched with coffee stains. Lord knows how long it had been sitting in his pocket.

"I found Vic when he was waiting tables at IHOP. And now look at him. Now he's waiting tables at some fancy restaurant on Melrose. And soon he won't even need to do that anymore." His round face shone with pleasure. "Any day now, my Vic is gonna be a star!"

Just then, the comics at the bar started whispering excitedly as Spiro ushered a chiseled blonde in an Armani suit to a ringside table.

"Look," I heard one of them say, "it's Regan Dixon."

I had no idea who Regan Dixon was, but whoever she was, I'd bet my bottom Pop-Tart she was important.

Vic finished his act to enthusiastic applause.

"He's not so damn funny," Dorcas groused into her scotch. "If it weren't for Hank's jokes, he'd be nothing."

I looked over at Hank, who, like Dorcas, didn't seem to be taking much pleasure in Vic's triumph. I wondered if he resented Vic basking in the limelight while he sat back here in anonymity.

Up onstage, Vic bowed with false humility.

Then, after milking the applause for as long as possible, he held up his hand for silence.

"Hey, everybody. I've got some good news I want to share. I've just signed a network pilot deal. A deal I never would've gotten without my agent."

"Congratulations," I said, turning to Manny.

But Manny was scratching his comb-over, puzzled.

"Pilot deal? I didn't get him a pilot deal."

"That's right," Vic said, "I owe it all to my new agent, Regan Dixon. In fact, she's headed to New York tonight to finalize the deal. C'mon, Regan. Stand up and take a bow."

The Armani beauty got up and waved to the audience, her white blond hair shining like a halo in the club's hazy air.

Meanwhile, next to me, Manny Vernon's face was a most unsettling shade of gray.

"Are you okay?" I asked.

But he just sat there, staring straight ahead, in a state of shock.

Vic made his way back to the bar, smug with victory, smiling and nodding as his fellow comics showered him with insincere congratulations.

At which point Manny sprang to life and grabbed Vic by the elbow.

"You little ingrate!" he shouted, obviously having regained his powers of speech. "After all I've done for you, you're walking out on me?"

"Afraid so," Vic said, shrugging free from his grasp.

"But you can't leave me," Manny wailed. "We've got a contract."

"That's what you think. It expired last week."

Manny blinked, confused.

"It did?"

"That's why you don't have any clients," Vic sneered. "Too many senior moments, pal. Time to pack it in and think about assisted living."

Manny crumpled back down on his bar stool as if he'd just been punched in the gut.

"How could you, Vic?" Allison had pushed her way through the circle of comics and was looking up at Vic in disbelief. "How could you fire Manny, after everything he's done for you?"

"Allie, baby, if I stuck with him, I'd be waiting tables all my life. It's a tough world. You gotta break some eggs to make an omelet."

Break eggs? This guy would break *legs* to get ahead.

"I'm long overdue for some changes in my life, Allie. In fact, I've got something I need to tell you."

At the edge of the crowd, Pebbles's eyes lit up in anticipation.

"It's about time," I heard her say.

Omigod, was Vic really going to dump Allison for this bimbette?

No, as it turned out, he was going to dump Allison for someone else, someone several notches higher on the food chain. As we were about to witness when Regan the megaagent joined the happy little crowd at the bar and linked her arm through Vic's.

"You killed 'em honey," she said, planting a kiss on his lips.

"Guess what, everybody?" Vic announced. "Regan and I are engaged."

Now it was Allison's turn to be speechless.

"Sorry about that, babe," Vic said to Allison, with a shrug. "I'm driving Regan to the airport to catch the red-eye. I'll come back to the house afterward and get my things."

A beat of shocked silence descended over the bar, a silence that was broken by the crash of broken glass.

Pebbles the barmaid had dropped her tray of drinks. She stood there, openmouthed, the words *Cute, but Psycho* practically pulsating with fury across her chest.

Then Allison burst into tears.

At the sight of those tears, Hank jumped off his bar stool and raced over to Vic.

"You piece of slime. How could you do this to her?"

The veins were throbbing in his scrawny neck.

"What are you complaining about?" Vic said. "I'm doing you a favor, buddy. You've always had the hots for Allison. Now's your chance."

Hank blushed furiously and took a wild swing at Vic. Clearly, Hank had never been on his high school boxing team. He missed by a mile. Vic grabbed Hank's arm and pinned it behind his back.

"You don't really want to do this, do you, buddy?"

Hank thought it over and, flushed with shame, shook his head no.

Vic smirked and let him go.

"Get yourself another writer," Hank said, rubbing his arm where Vic had twisted it. "I quit."

"Boo hoo," Vic said. "I'm shaking in my shoes. Writers are a dime a dozen."

"You're gonna need one," Hank countered, "if you keep using clichés like that."

"C'mon, Sugar Buns," Vic said, brushing past Hank and putting his arm around his trophy agent. "Let's get out of here."

Sugar Buns? Had Vic just called this power broker of a woman *Sugar Buns*? Surely, she'd object. But no, she just smiled up at him lovingly. Vic had obviously worked his magic on her, just as he had on Allison and Pebbles.

The happy couple headed for the exit when suddenly Dorcas, who'd been silent up to now, erupted like a long dormant volcano. With a guttural roar, she shoved her bar stool aside and charged across the room.

Before anyone could stop her, she jumped on Vic, tackling him from behind. He tried to fight her off. But, unlike Hank, Dorcas wasn't that easy to get rid of. Propelled by rage, she was surprisingly strong. Within seconds she'd wrestled Vic to the ground and was sitting on his chest, her hands around his neck.

"You worthless excuse for a human being!" she bellowed. "You've hurt enough people on this planet. You don't deserve to live one minute longer."

Then she began strangling him.

Vic lay trapped beneath her, gasping for air, but Dorcas was oblivious, her hands locked in a viselike grip around his neck.

"Oh, my God!" Regan cried out. "Somebody stop her!"

"Yeah," Spiro said, racing over to the fracas. "I'm not insured for this kind of thing."

Funny how nobody else was all that eager to save him.

Finally, Pete the bartender said, "Oh, well, I suppose somebody's gotta do it," and leapt over the bar.

But he needn't have bothered.

At that moment, Dorcas released her grip on Vic's neck. She stared down at her hands, puzzled, as if waking from a bad dream. Whatever rage had taken hold of her had drained away. The volcano was dormant again.

Vic, however, was not nearly so calm.

He glared at her with undisguised loathing.

"You're going to regret this," he hissed.

And indeed, she would.

No way was I going to let Dorcas drive home; the woman had chugalugged enough scotch to open her own distillery.

"C'mon," I said, as I led out her outside, "let's walk over to Pinky's and get some coffee."

"Wait!" She stumbled over the doorjamb. "I forgot my idea book."

Her "idea book" was a loose-leaf binder filled with half-baked notions for her act. She'd taken it out for our work session, only to ignore it with the arrival of her first scotch.

"I'll go get it," I said.

I propped her up against the door and hurried back inside.

A desperate comic was struggling onstage for the audience's attention but nobody was listening; most of them were still buzzing about the dramatic scene they'd just witnessed.

At the bar, Manny was staring morosely into a glass of cream soda. Allison, her face blotchy with tears, was sitting with Hank, who held her hand, patting it sympathetically. Although the expression on his face was one of concern, I couldn't help but notice a look of longing in his eyes. I thought about what Vic had said, that he was doing Hank a favor by breaking up with Allison, and wondered if Hank was secretly happy at this recent turn of events.

I headed over to where Dorcas had been sitting. Her idea book was on the bar where she'd left it.

Pebbles the barmaid was behind the bar, taking a surreptitious slug of beer.

As I reached for the notebook, I heard her say to Pete, "Too bad she didn't go through with it."

"Yeah," Pete laughed. "For once Dorcas gave people something they wanted to see."

I returned to the entrance and picked up Dorcas where I'd left her, still propped up against the door. Somehow I managed to steer her over to Pinky's, where I spent the next hour pouring coffee and bacon and eggs into her, waiting for her to sober up. On the plus side, I finally had an order of those fries I'd been lusting after all evening.

"I don't know what got into me," Dorcas kept moaning.

Three double scotches and a strawberry margarita, that's what.

"Vic got me so mad," she said, spearing a piece of bacon, "something inside me just snapped."

"I understand."

Frankly, I didn't blame her for what she did. Not the strangling part, of course. But the knocking Vic to the ground and putting the fear of God in him part. He needed a dose of that.

"You should've seen the look on his face," she said, sopping up the last of her eggs with a piece of toast. "For once, the little rat looked scared."

Then she grinned.

"True confession: It felt great."

"I'll bet it did."

She sat up straight. All that coffee and animal fat seemed to have revived her.

"I was a fool to let Vic get to me. Some day he'll be punished for all the rotten things he's ever done. I believe that what goes around comes around. Don't you, Jaine?"

I couldn't have disagreed with her more. Plenty of people

went unpunished for their sins. People like Lucrezia Borgia, Ivan the Terrible, and the guy who invented spandex bike shorts, to name just a few.

But I just smiled and nodded.

"Meanwhile," she said, "I'm going to show Vic how funny I can be. I'm going to show everybody." By now her eyes were shining with determination. "I'm going to be a star, Jaine. And you're going to help me!"

Talk about your Mission Impossible.

I signaled to the waitress.

"Check, please."

I walked Dorcas back to her car, then forked over five bucks I couldn't afford to retrieve Wheezy from the wise guy teenage valet.

"You going to be driving it home?" he smirked. "Or pedaling?"

By the time I staggered home to my apartment, I knew there was no way on earth I could work for Dorcas. I simply couldn't make her funny. Not without a brain transplant.

I'd have to turn down the job. So what if I didn't have the money for a new car? If I had to ride around town on a bicycle, so be it. All I needed was an excuse, some way to let Dorcas down gently. Maybe I'd tell her I was entering a convent. Or going on an unexpected honeymoon. Or joining the peace corps and moving to the Fiji Islands.

Okay, so they weren't exactly believable, but it was after midnight, and I was exhausted.

But I needn't have bothered thinking up excuses. As I was about to learn the next morning, I wasn't going to have to write jokes for Dorcas after all.

Not unless she planned on doing her act from jail.

YOU'VE GOT MAIL!

To: Jausten
From: DaddyO
Subject: Good Luck Gone Forever

Dearest Lambchop—

Now that Mom has given away my lucky shirt, my life is a shambles. Here's a list of what's gone wrong in the past twenty-four hours:

My computer crashed.

I lost eighteen holes of miniature golf to Ed Peters.

I sat on my prescription sunglasses.

And you know how I've always had great luck finding parking spaces? Not anymore. I can't find a parking space to save my soul. Yesterday I had to park five blocks away from the post office when I went to mail you that painting of dogs playing poker.

What can I say, lambchop? Thanks to your mom, my good luck is gone forever.

Your desolate,
Daddy

To: Jausten
From: Shoptillyoudrop
Subject: It's All in His Mind

Jaine, darling—

Daddy has been driving me crazy! He's convinced that he's living under a black cloud of bad luck. Of course, it's all in his mind.

I sneaked a peek at the e-mail he wrote you, and it's all nonsense!

First off, his computer didn't really crash. When the repairman came out to fix it, he discovered that Daddy had accidentally knocked one of the cables loose. That's all. Nothing was broken. The big computer "crash" was just Daddy being his usual clumsy self!

And all that moaning and groaning about losing at miniature golf to Ed Peters. Ed always beats him at miniature golf. That's what started the whole Sunday brunch food fight that got Daddy kicked out of the clubhouse. Now Daddy's convinced himself that he never lost to Ed when he was wearing his "lucky" shirt.

And I don't care what he says. Daddy's never had any luck finding parking spaces. Why, he'll circle around till he practically wears out his tires before he finally breaks down and pulls into a parking lot.

As for his prescription sunglasses, Daddy's always sitting on them. In fact, the last time he sat on them, he was wearing his "lucky" shirt!

But worst of all is something Daddy didn't write about. He's convinced he's lost his ability to "perform" in the boudoir.

You know I don't like to talk about these kinds of things with you, darling, but you can guess what that means—no dipsy doodle.

Oh, dear. If only I hadn't given away that silly shirt of his.

Your frazzled,
Mom

P.S. I sent away for a male potency vitamin from the Shopping Channel called "Vita-Mans." They're Fed-Exing it overnight. Maybe that'll help.

Chapter 7

I almost choked on my rice cake when I saw the headline in the paper the next morning:

LOCAL COMIC STRANGLED WITH CONTROL-TOP PANTYHOSE
ANGRY RIVAL ARRESTED AT SCENE OF THE CRIME

Under the headline was a publicity photo of Vic, baring his teeth at the camera in a chemically whitened grin.

According to the paper, after he drove Regan to the airport for her red-eye to New York, he returned home to the bungalow he shared with Allison and started packing his belongings. Only he never finished. Somewhere between his dress shirts and his jockey shorts, he got murdered.

The cops found him sprawled out in the living room, strangled with a pair of pantyhose. What's more, they found the apparent murderer kneeling over him, still clutching the pantyhose.

And that apparent murderer was Dorcas.

I blinked in disbelief. When I last left Dorcas, she was upbeat and hopeful. What on earth had happened? Instead of going home to plan her rise to stardom, she'd obviously decided to switch to Plan B and strangle Vic instead.

"Omigosh," I said to Prozac, who was hard at work sniffing her genitals. "The comic I was working for just got arrested for murder."

Whatever. Got any anchovies?

Shaken by the news, I headed to the kitchen for a refill on my coffee and another rice cake. (Okay, so it wasn't a rice cake. It was a cinnamon raisin bagel. With butter. And jelly, too, if you must know.)

Not that I was surprised that Vic had been killed. This was a guy begging to be murdered. I just had a hard time believing Dorcas did it. True, she'd almost strangled him at the club. But I remembered the look of bewilderment on her face when she realized what she'd just done. She simply didn't seem like a cold-blooded killer to me.

Then it occurred to me that with Dorcas in jail, at least I wouldn't have to write jokes for her. But on the minus side, it meant I was back at square one, in desperate need of a writing assignment.

So reluctantly I put Dorcas out of my mind and shuffled over to my computer to look for work. I checked the postings on Monster and *Adweek*. Nothing. Not unless I wanted to be a fry cook, a scuba instructor, or a male exotic dancer.

With a weary sigh, I opened my parents' e-mails. What did I tell you? I knew Daddy would drive Mom crazy over that silly shirt.

I blushed when I read the part about their "dipsy doodle" problems. I couldn't imagine my parents having dipsy doodle, let alone having problems. In fact, all medical and biological evidence to the contrary, I prefer to believe that I was brought into this world by a cartoon stork.

But I couldn't worry about my parents and their newly acquired dependence on Vita-Mans. Not now. Not with "Buy a Car" at the top of my To Do list.

Then, just as I popped the last of the bagel in my mouth, I

had a brainstorm. Why not call Andrew Ferguson? After all, his bank had offered me a job last year; maybe they had something available now.

I reached for the phone but then got cold feet. What if Andrew thought I was using my job search as an excuse to call him? I didn't want to look like a dating desperado. Which I was, of course. But still, I didn't want to look like one. Oh, who cared what I looked like? I needed a job, and I needed it badly. Appearances be damned.

I picked up the phone and dialed.

"Union National," a receptionist chirped.

"Andrew Ferguson, please."

I was on hold listening to a spiel about Union National's friendly personal service when a clipped secretary's voice came on the line.

"Sam Weinstock's office."

Damn. The last person I wanted to talk to was Sam.

"I must have the wrong extension. I was looking for Andrew Ferguson."

"You have the right extension. He's working with Ms. Weinstock. Whom shall I say is calling?"

And that moment I knew as sure as Reese's made Pieces that I'd never get a job at Union National. Not as long as Sam Weinstock was CFO. I saw those dagger looks she gave me in the restaurant. She'd never hire anyone who was a possible rival for Andrew's affections.

"Never mind," I said and hung up.

I speared some bagel crumbs with a wet fingertip and considered my options. I'd called all my current clients and all my former clients. None of them had any work for me. There was only one thing left to do: the thing I dreaded most in the world, aside from stepping on the scale in the doctor's office—making cold calls. Yes, I'd have to call and pitch my services to every ad agency and PR firm in the city.

It was a grueling job, but it had to be done.

So I squared my shoulders, gathered my courage, and spent the next several hours watching daytime TV. What can I say? I couldn't face the prospect of trying to talk my way past secretaries trained like guard dogs to ward off job hunters like me.

I was lolling on the sofa, wishing I had some of Oprah's spunk (not to mention some of her money), when the local news came on.

The top story was Dorcas's arrest. Her lawyer, a court-appointed attorney named Dickie Partridge, stood outside police headquarters talking to reporters. Or, I should say, mumbling to reporters. He had all the confidence of me appearing in public in a bathing suit.

Dickie was just a kid, probably five minutes out of law school. With a freckled face and red hair dotted with cowlicks, he looked like he should've been in study hall doing his algebra homework. He stammered into the mike, feebly insisting that his client was innocent, about as dynamic as a wet sponge.

With this guy defending her, Dorcas was in deep doo doo.

For a fleeting instant, I thought about offering to investigate on her behalf. You'd never believe it to look at me in my elastic-waist pants and *Cuckoo for Cocoa Puffs* T-shirt, but I've actually managed to solve a few murders in my lifetime, murders you can read all about in my Pulitzer Prize–winning books listed at the front of this book. (Okay, so I never actually wrote a Pulitzer Prize–winning book, but I've read a few. Does that count?)

Yes, I thought about calling Dorcas, but not for long. I simply couldn't afford to get involved in the case. I'd been crazy to take her slave-wage job in the first place. Besides, for all I knew, maybe she really did kill Vic. After all, she came *thisclose* to strangling him at the club.

And maybe I was wrong about her attorney. Maybe he was a budding Clarence Darrow and would have her ripping her pantyhose to shreds in front of booing audiences in no time.

No, I had to forget about Dorcas, and start making those cold calls.

And so, with the fierce stick-to-it-iveness that I'm famous for, I picked up the phone and dialed.

"County jail?" I said. "I'd like to make arrangements to visit one of your prisoners."

"*You're* a detective?"

Dorcas sat across from me in the visitors room of the L.A. County Women's Jail (better known to its feminine felons as the Sybil Brand Institute). She looked skinnier than ever, lost in the folds of an unflattering orange jumpsuit.

"I don't understand." She spoke into a phone behind the bulletproof divider that separated us. "I thought you were a writer."

"I do some private detective work on the side," I said into my phone, wondering what sort of person had used the phone before me, hoping it wasn't a hepatitis C kind of person.

Dorcas was staring at me, still a bit dubious.

"Isn't it hard to chase down criminals when you're as out of shape as you are?"

Okay, she didn't really say that, but I could tell from the look of incredulity in her eyes that she was thinking something along those lines.

"So you're really a private eye?" were the words that actually came out of her mouth.

I nodded.

"And you've come here to help me?"

"That depends."

"On what?"

"Did you kill Vic?"

"Of course not!"

I figured she was telling the truth. I'd seen her act. She wasn't that good a performer to lie so convincingly.

"In that case," I said, "I'm here to help."

"I can't afford to pay you much. In fact, now that I'm in jail and not working, I can't afford to pay you anything."

Drat. I was hoping for something. A tiny pittance to at least cover my expenses.

I guess she could see the look of disappointment on my face, because the next thing she said was: "Of course, I could always cash in my savings bond."

Go ahead, I told myself. Let her cash in her savings bond. People cashed in their bonds all the time. It wouldn't kill her. I couldn't afford to work on this case for nothing. I wasn't running a charity.

"No," I said, "I can't let you do that."

I know. I've got the backbone of a caterpillar. But she looked so pathetic sitting there in that ghastly orange jumpsuit, I couldn't let her cash in what was probably her life's savings.

"Oh, Jaine!" Her eyes lit up with gratitude. "How can I ever thank you?"

Money might've been nice, but I'd just talked myself out of that little treat.

"I need all the help I can get," she said. "The cops are convinced I killed Vic, and my lawyer's just a kid. When he came to visit me, I swear I saw a tube of Clearasil in his attaché case. He told me this was his first murder case."

It was hard to see clearly through the fingerprint smudges on the Plexiglas divider, but I thought I saw a tear rolling down Dorcas's cheek.

"Oh, God," she said, "I'm going to spend the rest of my life in jail for a crime I didn't commit."

Now there was no doubt about it; tears were streaming down her face.

"Please, Dorcas. Don't cry. I'll get you out of this," I promised rashly. "But first you have to tell me what happened. What on earth were you doing at Vic's bungalow last night?"

She wiped her nose on her orange sleeve and, after a deep, shuddery breath began to talk.

"I was on a high when I left you at Pinky's. But by the time I drove home, I was depressed all over again. All my optimism flew out the window somewhere between the deli and my apartment. I was convinced that Vic was right, and that I was never going to make it in show business. So I broke open a bottle of Bailey's Irish Cream left over from Christmas, and the next thing I knew I was drunk again. I don't know if you noticed, but I don't handle my liquor very well."

Yep, I noticed. I would have to be in a coma not to.

"I got to thinking about Vic and all the rotten things he ever did to me, and the next thing I knew I was back in my car driving over to his bungalow in Venice."

"How did you know where he lived?"

"His address is in the phone book. Anybody could look it up. But I didn't have to. I already knew where he lived. It wasn't the first time I'd made that trip. I'd wanted to tell him off lots of times."

She took another pass at her nose with the sleeve of her jumpsuit.

"When I got there, I knocked on the door but there was no answer. I must've stood outside ten minutes banging on the door. Then I tried the knob and discovered that the door was open.

"So I walked in. It was dark inside. I saw a lump in the

middle of the living room. At first I didn't know what it was, but as I got closer I saw it was Vic. He was sprawled on the floor with a pair of pantyhose around his neck."

She shuddered at the memory.

"I wasn't sure he was dead, so I bent down to untie the pantyhose. That's when the cops showed up. I guess I'd made a racket banging on the door, and one of the neighbors called the police.

"And that's how they found me, kneeling over Vic's dead body, holding the murder weapon. And it turns out the pantyhose is the exact same kind I use in my act.

"But I swear, Jaine," she said, her eyes once more welling with tears, "I didn't do it. Vic was dead when I got there. You've got to believe me."

And I did.

There were plenty of people with stronger motives to kill Vic than Dorcas. There was Allison, his jilted girlfriend. And Manny, his jilted agent. Not to mention Pebbles, his jilted lover.

Any one of them could've swiped a pair of pantyhose from Dorcas's tote bag. All eyes were on Dorcas when she attacked Vic at the club that night. Nobody was looking at her bag. It would have been easy for someone to slip over and lift the pantyhose. Someone who planned to take advantage of Dorcas's outburst and frame her for murder.

"I don't understand why the cops are so certain you did it," I said. "Vic had an enemies list longer than Nixon's."

"I know. But he was killed with my pantyhose. And a club full of witnesses saw me try to strangle him earlier that night."

"Yes, but if you were the killer, why would you incriminate yourself with a pair of your own pantyhose?"

"I guess the cops must think I'm pretty stupid."

"I still don't see how they can be so sure it's you. Believe me, if you had a better lawyer, you wouldn't be sitting in jail right now."

"There's something else," she said. "Something I haven't told you. Remember that ex-wife Vic made fun of in his act?"

I nodded.

"Well," she sighed, "that ex-wife is me."

Chapter 8

I was so flabbergasted, I almost dropped the phone.

"You were married to Vic?"

She nodded. "Six years ago in New Jersey. I met him at a comedy club. We were both doing stand-up. I know it's hard to believe, but he was really very sweet. He's always sweet in the beginning. It's not until he's through with you that you see his ugly side."

"Five more minutes!" I looked up and saw a prison guard the size of a Hummer checking her watch.

Dorcas sighed, and continued her tale. "I knew right away Vic was a better performer than I was. So I gave up my act and started writing jokes for him."

Dorcas? A joke writer? I found that hard to believe. The woman was about as funny as toe fungus.

"I was a lot funnier back then," she said, as if reading my thoughts. "Anyhow, soon after we were married, we decided to move to L.A. We weren't here three weeks when I caught Vic sleeping with another woman, a flight attendant in our apartment building. He promised he'd never see her again. And he kept his word. He dumped her and started dating her roommate."

She laughed bitterly.

"Six months later, the marriage was over. He left me for a

massage therapist and fired me as his writer. He said the only reason he'd ever used my jokes in the first place was because they were free."

"What a prince."

"For weeks, I was crushed. I must've lost at least twenty pounds."

I eyed Dorcas with envy. True, she was in jail and about to be tried for murder, but on the plus side, she was one of those lucky women who lose weight when they're miserable.

"Then one day I stopped being sad and got mad. I decided to start doing my act again. I vowed that someday I'd be famous and Vic would be sorry. Only somewhere along the line, I'd lost my confidence. I wasn't funny anymore. And even though Vic couldn't write a joke to save his life, he was good onstage. People liked him. He kept doing well, and I kept bombing."

I knew only too well how badly Dorcas could bomb.

"You'd think he'd feel sorry for me after the way he'd treated me, but no. Vic loved to see me fail. You saw how he kept riding me. He was merciless. With each insult, he chipped away what was left of my confidence, until it was completely gone. He ruined me, and I hated him for it.

"But I swear I didn't kill him. I couldn't. I think there was even a part of me that still loved him." She shook her head in wonder. "Talk about sick, huh?"

But I didn't have time to comment on her neuroses. Because just then the Hummer guard came over and tapped her on the shoulder. Visiting hours were over.

I drove home, stunned. So Dorcas was Vic's ex-wife. His angry ex-wife. No wonder the cops arrested her. And yet, my gut told me she was innocent. Of course, my gut has been known to mislead me on occasion. (It still insists that cheesecake isn't fattening.)

I let myself into my apartment and tossed my mail on the dining room table. Prozac, who'd been napping on my computer keyboard, woke up and began wailing for food. Poor darling hadn't eaten in two whole hours. I stumbled into the kitchen, trying to not step on her as she darted in and out between my ankles, the way she does when she's helping me prepare a snack.

I gave her some Krunchy Karp Treats and grabbed a handful of Cocoa Puffs for myself.

I was just about to settle down and plot out my investigation when the doorbell rang. I opened the door and found Lance on my doorstep.

"Hi, Jaine. I heard you come home."

Which is no surprise. With his borderline X-ray hearing, Lance hears just about everything that goes on in my apartment. (And your apartment, too, if you live anywhere near us.)

He strolled inside, as he always does, without waiting for an invitation.

"The UPS man came while you were gone," he said, handing me a package from the shopping channel. "Another outfit from your mom?"

I nodded wearily. "A sequined palm tree shorts set."

He winced in pain.

"You realize, of course, that wearing it is out of the question."

"Don't worry," I said. "I'll give it to charity. Know any needy drag queens?"

"Afraid not."

He picked up my mail and began shuffling through it.

"So how'd things go on your lunch date?"

"I'm not sure. Andrew said he'd call me for dinner but I haven't heard from him."

"You didn't unbutton your waistband, did you?"

"Of course not," I lied.

"It's only been a few days. Give him a chance. Hey, what's this?" he asked, holding up a piece of mail. "You've got a letter from Gustavo Mendes."

"Who's Gustavo Mendes?"

He shot me a look of disbelief.

"Jaine, don't you know anything? He's only the hottest new hairstylist in L.A."

"Well, excuse me. I guess I must've been filling my head with unimportant stuff like suicide bombings in the Middle East and famine in Somalia."

He ripped it open and began reading.

"No," I said, "I don't mind if you read my personal mail. Go right ahead."

"Listen to this," he said, ignoring my feeble attempt at sarcasm. "They're giving you a free styling." He read aloud from the letter: "Because you're an influential contributor to the local media, we're hoping you'll let us treat you to a complimentary cut and color at our new Santa Monica salon."

He looked up from the letter, puzzled.

"Since when are you an influential contributor to the media?"

"I guess they must've seen my story in the *Times* on 24-hour Botox centers and assumed I have some actual influence in this town. If they only knew I write toilet bowl ads for a living."

"What they don't know won't hurt them," he said, grabbing my phone. "You've got to call this minute and make an appointment."

"No, I don't. Fancy salons intimidate me. And besides, I don't have time to get my hair done. I've got a murder to investigate."

"Again?"

"Yeah. A comic I was supposed to be writing jokes for just got arrested for murder."

"You mean the Pantyhose Murderer? It's all over the news."

I nodded.

He shook his blond curls in disapproval.

"Jaine, if you spent more time at hair salons and less time around demented killers, you'd have a Significant Other by now."

Look who's talking, I thought. A guy whose flus last longer than his relationships.

"I'd better get going," he said, "or I'll be late for work. Big sale on designer running shoes. It's going to be a madhouse. Want me to pick up something for you?"

"A shoelace, maybe. That's all I can afford right now."

Lance tootled off, and I settled down on the sofa to figure out where to start my investigation. After a bit more thought, and a lot more Cocoa Puffs, I decided to pay a visit to Dorcas's freckle-faced attorney, Dickie Partridge, to find out what he knew about the case. I assumed that by now he'd had a chance to talk with the cops. I would've gone to the cops myself, but past experience has shown they're not always willing to share information with lady P.I.s in elastic-waist pants.

I looked up Dickie's address in the Yellow Pages. His phone number, I noted, was 1-800-UR NOCNT.

I hoped he litigated better than he spelled.

Dickie's office was in a rundown "professional" building not far from the jail, filled with bail bondsmen and discount dentists, as well as a few professionals in hot pants plying their trade on the sidewalk out front.

I took a rickety elevator up to the third floor, then made my way to the end of a dank corridor till I came to a door that said: *Dickie Partridge, Esquire.*

You have to wonder about an attorney who calls himself "Dickie." It's like a neurosurgeon calling himself Skippy. Doesn't exactly inspire confidence, does it?

I knocked on the door and heard a muffled, "Come in."

Inside, Dickie sat at his desk, looking very much as I'd seen him on TV: Same Opie of Mayberry freckled face. Same unruly cowlicks. If anything, he looked younger and more inexperienced in person.

His lunch was spread out in front of him: a plastic tub of Spaghetti-O's, carrot sticks, and a carton of milk with a straw.

I was surprised he didn't have a lunch box.

"I was just having my lunch," he said, gulping down some Spaghetti-O's. "Care for a carrot stick?"

"No, thanks."

Somehow I can always Just Say No to carrot sticks.

"Please, sit down," he said, gesturing to the only chair in the room.

I took a seat, and as I did, the phone rang. Dickie picked it up eagerly.

"Dickie Partridge, Esquire," he said, his voice ripe with expectation.

"Oh." His face fell. "Hi, Mom. . . . Yes, I am. Right now, in fact . . . No, I won't forget to eat the carrot strips. . . . Yes, I promise I'll call if I'm going to be late."

He hung up and rolled his eyes.

"I'm living with my folks until I can find a place of my own. You don't happen to know of a one-bedroom apartment for about $250 a month, do you?"

Was he kidding? For two-fifty a month, he was going to have to move out of the city. Way out of the city. Say, to the Philippines.

"Sorry, I'm afraid not."

"So how can I be of service?" he asked, clasping his hands

on his desk and trying to look like an actual attorney. A look he didn't quite achieve due to a not very lawyerly dab of Spaghetti-O sauce on his chin.

Before I could tell him how he could help me, the phone rang again. Once again, he reached for it eagerly only to be disappointed.

"What is it now, Mom?"

He spent the next few minutes on the phone, writing a list of grocery items he was supposed to pick up on his way home from work. While Dickie took dictation, I got up and checked out the framed law degree on his wall.

I blinked in surprise when I saw that it was from Harvard. Maybe Dickie wasn't such a dufus after all.

"I see you went to Harvard Law School," I said when he finally got off the phone. "That's very impressive."

"Um, actually, it's not Harvard."

"It isn't?"

"No, it's *Harvad*."

I took another look. Indeed, there was a pivotal "r" missing in Harvad.

"Harvad? I've never heard of that school."

"It's on the internet."

I gulped.

"Fully accredited, though."

Oh, dear. Dorcas was in deep doo doo, all right.

"So how can I be of service?" He smiled eagerly, visions of legal fees dancing in his cowlicked head.

Now it was my turn to confess.

"Actually," I said, "I'm not a client."

"Oh." His smile faded.

"I'm a part-time private eye, a friend of Dorcas's. I wanted to see how her case is coming along."

He instantly cheered up at the mention of Dorcas.

"Great!" he beamed. "Just great. With any luck, she should be out of jail in ten years! I'm going to have her plead temporary insanity."

"You can't let her do that. She didn't do it."

"But they found her standing over the body with the murder weapon."

"I don't care how they found her. She's innocent. And I intend to prove it. That's why I'm here. I'm hoping you can share some insider information with me. Like, for instance, what have the cops told you so far?"

"Nothing." He sighed. "They won't return my calls."

"How about the DA's office?"

"Nope. Haven't heard from them, either."

Rats. This guy was about as helpful as a migraine.

"Sure you wouldn't like a carrot strip?" he offered, as a consolation prize.

I passed on the carrot strip and headed back outside.

It looked like I'd be flying solo on this case, I thought, wending my way past the hookers out front.

I got in Wheezy and sat there for a while, watching the hookers tug at their hot pants, and trying to figure out what to do next.

Finally I made up my mind.

I'd go back to where all the trouble began—at the Laff Palace.

The Laff Palace looked even scuzzier in broad daylight than it had at night. Which pretty damn near broke the needle on the scuzzy-o-meter. As I drove into the nearly deserted parking lot, I saw paint peeling from the "palace" walls and shingles missing from the roof.

I'd forgotten that the club would be closed during the day. But luckily I saw Spiro's sports car in the parking lot. At least

I assumed it was Spiro's car from the license plate, which read MR LAFF.

I rang the bell and Spiro came to the door in his electric-blue jumpsuit, a boatload of gold chains nestled in his chest hair. Like the Laff Palace, he looked a lot worse in the light of day.

"Yeah?" He squinted into the sun. "What do you want?"

"I'm investigating Vic Cleveland's murder," I said, trying to sound as *Law & Order*ish as possible.

His eyes narrowed.

"You a cop?"

I got the distinct impression he wasn't fond of cops.

"No," I hastened to assure him. "I'm a private eye."

"Is that so?" He looked me up and down. "You sure don't look like one."

"Well, I am," I said, wishing I'd remembered to change out of my *Cuckoo for Cocoa Puffs* T-shirt.

"Wait a minute," he said, scratching a patch of scalp between his hair plugs. "Didn't I see you here the other night with Dorcas?"

"Yes, I'm her writer. That is, I was her writer. Now I'm investigating on her behalf."

"Aren't you the busy little bee? Well, lotsa luck, sweetheart. You're gonna need it."

With that, he started to shut the door in my face.

"Wait!" I shoved my bag in the crack before he could close it completely. "I can prove Dorcas didn't kill Vic, but I need your help."

That piqued his interest.

"You can prove Dorcas didn't kill Vic? How?"

"Let me in and I'll tell you."

Curiosity got the better of him and he opened the door.

I followed him past the deserted stage down the corridor

to his office. With the houselights on, I could see the place was just a cockroach away from being condemned by the board of health. I thanked my lucky stars I hadn't ordered those Laff Palace fries.

Spiro ushered me to his office, a cheesy box of a room with fake wood-paneled walls and orange shag carpeting so moldy, it was probably sprouting mushrooms.

It didn't take a rocket scientist to figure out that Spiro—with his gold chains, Rolex, and a humungous diamond pinkie ring—was spending all his profits on himself, not on his business.

"Have a seat," he said, pointing to a hard metal chair stolen, no doubt, from a Knights of Columbus banquet hall.

I sat down and looked around. The walls were lined with photos of Spiro posing with every comic known to man. There was Spiro with Leno, Spiro with Letterman, Spiro with Joan Rivers, Ray Romano, Jerry Seinfeld, George Carlin, and Margaret Cho. The scary thing was that he seemed to be wearing the same godawful jumpsuit in every picture. I wondered, with a shudder, if it had ever been laundered.

On his desk was a framed photo of a frumpy woman with a faint mustache smiling stiffly at the camera. Mrs. Spiro, I presumed.

"So," he said, propping his Gucci loafers on his particle board desk, "how can you prove Dorcas didn't kill Vic?"

"I can't prove it beyond a shadow of a doubt," I admitted, "but I think the killer stole a pair of Dorcas's pantyhose and used them to strangle Vic and frame Dorcas for the murder."

"That's quite a theory," he said, buffing his pinky ring on his chest.

"All eyes were riveted on Dorcas when she was attacking Vic. Anyone could've sneaked over and lifted a pair of hose from her tote bag."

Including Spiro.

I remembered how he came racing over to Dorcas after she attacked Vic, shouting for someone to call the police. But it had taken him a while to get there. Where had he been at the beginning of her attack? At the bar, pilfering a pair of pantyhose?

Could Spiro possibly be the killer? He was the ideal murder suspect. An oily character with a face only a mug shot could love. But what on earth was his motive?

"Anyhow," I said, "I was hoping that your security camera caught the culprit in action."

"Security camera? What security camera?"

"You don't have a security system?"

"Sweetheart," he said, reaching down behind his desk, "the only security device at the Laff Palace is this."

He lifted a huge baseball bat onto his desk.

"Somebody messes with me, and splat!"

He got up and swung the bat with ferocious force.

I made mental note to never, under any circumstances, mess with Spiro.

"Did you happen to see anybody near Dorcas's bag that night?" I asked, eager to change the subject.

"Only Dorcas," he said.

"And you," he added, with an oily grin.

"Other than Dorcas and me, do you have any idea who might have killed Vic?"

"Who knows?" He shrugged. "Lots of people hated Vic. He was a ruthless guy. That's what it takes to make it in this business. Personally I respected him. And I'm sorry he's dead."

Call me a gullible fool, but he seemed to mean it.

"And just for the record," he added, "I didn't knock him off."

He glared at me with beady brown eyes, defying me to challenge him. And I wasn't about to—not with that bat sitting on his desk.

Instead, I thanked him for his time and got the heck out of there.

Chapter 9

"**I** found the most wonderful actress to play me at traffic school!"

Kandi and I were sitting across from each other, sipping margaritas at our favorite restaurant, Paco's Tacos, an unpretentious Mexican joint with burritos the size of third world countries.

Kandi grinned, quite pleased with herself.

"Miranda's a fabulous actress, a graduate of Yale Drama School. And really smart. She's bound to ace the test."

She rummaged through the basket of chips on our table, searching for one without any flaws.

"Kandi, just take one," I said, grabbing a handful. "It doesn't matter if it's broken. It still tastes the same."

"I know, but I like to eat the perfect ones first."

She does the same thing with french fries. Watching her eat is like watching an archaeologist dig for fossils.

"If I do say so myself," she said, finally choosing a chip that met with her approval, "hiring Miranda was a fabulous idea. Like having a real-life stunt double. Someone to do all the disagreeable things in life I don't want to do."

She took a contemplative bite of her chip.

"Too bad I can't use her for teeth cleaning and mammograms."

At that moment, the waiter showed up with our dinners. I'd ordered my favorite, the Number 11, the chimichanga combo plate. Kandi had opted for the far more sensible tostada.

One look at my food, and my salivary glands sprang into action. Sitting on my enormous plate were two crispy chicken chimichangas topped with twin dollops of sour cream, surrounded by hearty portions of refried beans and rice.

I grabbed my fork and stabbed a hunk of chimichanga. But just as I was about to eat it, Kandi grabbed my wrist and shouted, "Wait!"

"What's wrong?" I looked at her, alarmed. Was there something wrong with the food? Had she seen a cucaracha in my chimichanga? But that couldn't be. Paco's always had an "A" rating from the board of health.

"You can't eat yet. I've got something to show you!"

She reached into her purse and whipped out a round device about the size of an egg timer.

"It's called a Slo-Eater," she said, plopping it on the table between us, "and it's the perfect diet aid."

"Kandi, you don't need a diet aid."

And she didn't. She's a perfect size six on a bloated day. Of course, that's the way it is with size sixes. They're always on the hunt for new ways to lose weight. While gals like me are always on the hunt for new toppings for our pizzas.

"It's supposed to slow down your eating," she said, "so your brain has time to tell your stomach it's full before you overeat. See the little light?" She pointed to a tiny light at the top of the device. "It blinks every thirty seconds, and every time it blinks, you're allowed to take another bite."

Great. Just what I needed. A Bite Nazi.

"Kandi," I sighed, "my brain and my stomach haven't been on speaking terms for decades. And they're not about to start talking now."

"You mean, you're not even going to try it?"

"Not with these chimichangas calling my name."

I plowed into my combination plate with gusto.

She shook her head in disapproval and took a Barbie-sized bite of her tostada.

"So tell me what's going on in your life," she said, killing time between bites. "Have they found your car?"

"No, not yet."

"You're better off if they don't. Who knows what kind of slobs have been riding around in it. They'll probably leave it littered with fast-food wrappers and ketchup stains. My car once got stolen and when I got it back I found dried bubble-gum stuck to the dashboard." She wrinkled her nose in disgust. "Some thieves are just so damn inconsiderate."

Ah, yes. If only car thieves cleaned up after themselves, the world would be a far more civilized place. But Kandi was right. If they ever found my Corolla, I'd probably have to take antibiotics just to sit in it again.

"So what else is new?" she asked, still in limbo between bites.

I decided not to tell her about the Pantyhose Murder. Kandi tends to worry about me, and I didn't want one of her scare-tactics lectures about the dangerous side effects of private detective work, like getting injured and/or killed.

So I told her about Andrew instead.

"Andrew Ferguson called. He's back from Germany."

Her eyes lit up. "The cutie from the bank?"

I nodded. "We had lunch the other day."

"What did you order? Nothing fattening, I hope."

What is it about me that turns my friends into nagging mother substitutes?

"Yes, as a matter of fact, I ordered a nice juicy burger with fries. Andrew says he likes a girl with a healthy appetite."

"That's what they all say. But when push comes to shove, what they really like is a girl who can bounce walnuts off her abs."

The light on the Slo-Eater flashed, and she took another bite of her tostada.

"When are you seeing him again?"

"He said he'd call to set up a dinner date."

"And has he?"

"Well, no."

She smiled smugly.

"My point, exactly. Really, Jaine. I'm only saying this because I love you and I want you to be happy, but you could stand to lose a pound or two."

It was true, of course. On both counts. I could stand to lose some weight. And she *was* only saying it because she loved me.

"Won't you give the Slo-Eater a try?" she pleaded.

By this time, I'd finished half my combo plate and Kandi hadn't even made it to her third bite of tostada.

"Okay," I sighed. "I'll try it."

Kandi was so happy, she forgot to take her next bite when the light flashed.

"You're going to love it," she squealed. "Not only do you lose weight, but you get to savor each bite. Now put a piece of food on your fork."

I cut off a healthy hunk of my remaining chimichanga.

"A smaller piece."

I shot her a dirty look and cut off a smaller piece.

"Now wait for the light to flash, and then you can eat it."

I sat there holding my fork halfway to my face waiting for the damn light to flash. I waited and waited, but nothing happened. After a while, I felt my fingers starting to cramp.

"This thing must be broken," I said. "Surely it should've flashed by now."

"Jaine, it's only been six seconds."

"It has to be longer than that."

"Now it's seven seconds. Only twenty-three more to go."

"Kandi, I'd like to finish this chimichanga before meno-pause."

"Surely you can wait twenty-three teeny little seconds, can't you?"

"No, as a matter of fact, I can't," I said, picking up the chimichanga and biting off a mouth-stuffing hunk.

Kandi exhaled a stream of disapproving tsk tsks.

"Don't you want to look thin for Andrew?"

"He's probably not going to call anyway."

Twenty minutes later, I'd finished my combo plate, a piece of flan, and after-dinner coffee.

Kandi was working on bite #7 of her tostada.

It's a good thing I love her so much; otherwise, I'd shoot her.

I was wrong about Andrew. Just as I was settling into bed that night with a good book and a warm cat, he called.

"Hope I'm not calling too late," he said. "Sam and I just got through working."

"No, it's not too late," I said, not exactly thrilled at the thought of Andrew and Sam working thigh by thigh until 10:30 at night.

"I was wondering if you're free for dinner tomorrow night," he said.

For once in my life I decided to play it cool.

"Gee, I don't know. Let me check my calendar to see if I've got anything scheduled."

Yeah, right. The only date I had scheduled was with the clown at the Jack in the Box. But I kept up the charade. I waited a few seconds (one-tenth of a bite in Kandi's new diet regime), then got back on the line.

"Yes, I can make it. Dinner sounds great."

"Wonderful. I'll pick you up around 7:30."

I hung up and turned to Prozac, who was curled up on my pillow.

"Guess what, Pro?" I said, scooping her up in my arms. "I'm having dinner with Andrew tomorrow night!"

Him again?

She wriggled free from my grasp.

Haven't you learned your lesson? Men are nothing but trouble.

Then she strutted to the edge of the bed.

"Where are you going?"

I'll be sleeping in the living room tonight.

"Don't be that way, Prozac."

This was the second time this week she was walking out on me. Why did I get the feeling that if she had opposable thumbs she'd be calling a divorce lawyer?

"If you stay, I'll bring you leftovers from the restaurant."

She shot me a baleful look.

Who do you think you're talking to? An alley cat? I can't be bribed with leftovers. A T-bone steak, maybe. A carton of moo shoo pork. A pepperoni pizza. But not leftovers.

Of course, she didn't really say all that, but I could tell by the angry swish of her tail that's what she was thinking. Then, with said tail held high, she headed out to the living room. I got out of bed and followed her.

"Prozac, you can't seriously be mad at me for going out on a date."

Let's put it this way. If I were you, I wouldn't put your feet in your slippers without checking for wet spots.

She jumped up on the sofa and began clawing my favorite throw pillow with a vengeance normally reserved for my pantyhose.

I headed back to bed, feeling a lot like a guest on a Jerry Springer show: "Single Women Who Cheat on Their Cats—And Live to Regret it."

YOU'VE GOT MAIL!

To: Jausten
From: Shoptillyoudrop
Subject: The Last Leaf

Oh, honey. It's been just awful. Daddy's been moping around the house, convinced he's cursed. (And he refuses to take the Vita-Mans; he says they give him indigestion.)

It's just like that O. Henry story, *The Last Leaf*, where a young girl is convinced she's going to die when the last leaf on a wall outside her window has died. It's all in her mind, of course, and her neighbor goes out and paints a leaf on a wall and saves her life.

Well, I decided to do the same thing. Not paint a leaf, of course. I'm such a terrible artist, and I doubt that would do any good, anyway.

But I decided to scour the city until I found a shirt just like Daddy's "lucky" Hawaiian shirt. I must've gone to every thrift shop and vintage clothing store in the greater Tampa area. I figured there had to be a shirt like Daddy's in a store somewhere.

I was wrong. I just about wore out my feet looking and came up empty-handed. Then, just when I was about to give up hope, I saw a homeless man wheeling a shopping cart, and he was wearing a shirt just like Daddy's! For a minute I thought it actually *was* Daddy's, that the homeless man had bought it at the thrift shop, but when I looked at it closely I saw it was in much better condition than Daddy's.

Everett, the homeless man, was a very nice fellow, just a little down on his luck, poor dear. I gave him twenty dollars for the shirt, and he was so grateful, he offered me half of the Twinkie he was eating, which was awfully nice of him. But Dr. May has ordered Daddy and me to cut down on sweets, so of course I said no.

I brought the shirt home and added a few ketchup stains, and now I'm going to tell Daddy that the thrift shop ladies called and said that they found his shirt, and then this whole horrible ordeal will be over!

Lots of love and kisses from your very relieved,
Mom

To: Jausten
From: DaddyO
Subject: Born Yesterday

Hi, lambchop—

Your mom tried to fool me by pretending she found my lucky shirt. But I wasn't born yesterday. I could tell right away it wasn't mine. It was missing my lucky gravy stain on the lapel. I'll never forget that stain. I got it the night I whupped Ed Peters' fanny at Pictionary.

Well, I guess I'll go fix myself a snack. Just keep your fingers crossed I don't have an accident on my way to the kitchen.

Your poor old,
Daddy

To: Jausten
From: Shoptillyoudrop
Subject: I'm So Mad, I Could Spit!

Argggh! I'm so mad, I could spit. After all the trouble I went to, Daddy knew right away the shirt wasn't his. All because of a stupid gravy stain. Good Lord. Your father can spill a glass of red wine on a white carpet and never notice it, but when it comes to a tiny speck of gravy on a hibiscus leaf, suddenly he's got X-ray vision.

When I think of that twenty dollars I spent for the shirt! Not to mention the $39.99 (plus shipping and handling!) I spent on those Vita-Mans. Oh, well. At least I did a good deed for Everett, the homeless fellow. Which is some small consolation.

As for Daddy, I give up. There's nothing else I can do except hope that this foolishness will pass. I can't wait till they let him back in the clubhouse. At least that will be a distraction.

Meanwhile, I've convinced him to go to the movies this afternoon. Anything to get him out of his darn recliner!

Hope you're a lot less stressed than I am, darling.

All my love—
Mom

Chapter 10

I'm happy to report there were no wet spots in my slippers the next morning. There was, however, a hairball the size of a cannoli on my dining room table.

But I had to count my blessings. At least I wasn't in Florida buying shirts from the homeless.

"Thanks loads," I said to Prozac, as I scooped up the hairball with a paper towel.

Don't mention it. She swished her tail and sashayed over to her food bowl.

"You're a spoiled brat; you know that, don't you?"

Can we skip the chatter and go straight to the main course?

I slopped some Luscious Lamb Guts into her bowl. She arched her back for her breakfast back rub, but she arched in vain. Two could play at this cold shoulder game.

I'd just finished washing up the remains of her hairball when I glanced down at yesterday's mail, still on the dining room table where I'd tossed it. And there on the top of the pile was the letter from Gustavo Mendes—according to Lance, L.A.'s hottest new hairstylist.

I picked up the letter and read it again. The stationery was impressively thick and creamy. And there, printed in a tasteful calligraphic typeface, was Gustavo's invitation to come in for a free hair styling.

Normally I tend to shy away from fancy salons where a cut and color costs more than a Kia. But the operative word here was *free*. Wouldn't it be nice to show up for my date with Andrew with spectacular hair?

What the heck, I thought, picking up the phone. I'd give them a call. Maybe they could squeeze me in.

But then as I dialed, I remembered it was Saturday. It had to be their busiest day of the week. They'd never be able to schedule me on such short notice.

But to my surprise, when I gave my name to the receptionist, she said, "Oh, Ms. Austen. What a pleasure. Yes, Gustavo will take you himself. How's three o'clock?"

Gustavo obviously had me confused with some other writer, someone vastly more important than the author of *In a Rush to Flush? Call Toiletmasters!* And I wasn't about to straighten him out. The only thing I wanted straightened were my unruly curls.

I quickly accepted the appointment before they could figure out the truth, and—thrilled at the prospect of a Fabulous Hair Day—ran to my closet and started trying on outfits for my date with Andrew.

I was standing there, trying to cram myself into a way-too-tight skirt I'd bought in a moment of optimistic madness, when I remembered Dorcas festering in jail.

Some private eye I was. (I bet Philip Marlowe never wasted valuable crime-solving time trying on outfits.) I promised Dorcas I'd find Vic's killer. Andrew or no Andrew, I had to live up to my promise and stay focused on the case.

Guiltily I wriggled out of the skirt and changed into elastic-waist jeans and a T-shirt. Then I looked up Vic's number in the phone book. His address was listed, just as Dorcas said it would be.

I grabbed my car keys and headed for the door.

"Bye, Pro," I called out to Prozac. But she didn't even bother to look up from the armchair she was clawing.

Minutes later, I was strapped in Wheezy lurching out to the Venice bungalow Vic had shared with Allison.

In other words, the scene of the crime.

Allison's house was on a tree-lined street in Venice, an unexpected haven of craftsman-style cottages, all built as summer getaways back in the early part of the last century.

Painted sky blue and surrounded by a white picket fence thick with cabbage roses, the tiny cottage was straight out of a storybook. I almost expected to see Rebecca of Sunnybrook Farm come bounding out the front door. From the minute I saw it, I thought of it as Allison's. I simply couldn't picture a slimeball like Vic living in a place this wholesome.

I let myself in through the picket gate and headed up a brick path. I could hear strains of a violin concerto coming from inside.

I rang the bell and seconds later I heard the muffled sound of footsteps.

Allison opened the door in a pair of pale pink pajamas, her Botticelli curls dishevelled, her eyes red rimmed from crying.

"I'm not talking to reporters," she said, wiping a stray curl from her brow.

"I'm not a reporter. I'm a private investigator."

"Sorry, I'm not giving interviews of any kind." She started to close the door and then stopped. "Didn't I see you the other night with Dorcas? Vic told me you were her writer."

I launched into my explanation of how I was indeed Dorcas's writer but also her private investigator. I waited for the inevitable *Funny, you don't look like a private eye*, but Allison scored major points with me by saying nothing along those lines.

"I promise I won't take long," I said, in my most soothing voice. "It's really very important."

I was afraid she might turn me away now that she knew I was working for the woman accused of killing her boyfriend, but to my relief, she sighed and said, "C'mon in."

I followed her through an arched doorway to the living room, a cozy space with a brick fireplace and overstuffed furniture.

"Have a seat," she said, plopping down onto her floral chintz sofa.

I sat across from her on a matching armchair, her violin case on the coffee table between us.

The concerto I'd heard coming up the path was playing on her stereo. She put her head back against the sofa and closed her eyes, lost in the music. I was beginning to wonder if she'd forgotten I was there, when she finally opened her eyes again.

"Sorry," she said, "I'm just so tired."

And she did look exhausted.

"I'd offer you some tea, but I don't have the energy to make it."

"Why don't I make some for us?"

"Would you mind?" She shot me a grateful smile.

"Not at all."

It would give me a chance to do a little snooping.

She pointed me in the direction of her kitchen, where, while waiting for the water to boil, I poked around in cupboards and drawers. Don't ask me what I expected to find. Fingerprints? DNA samples? A signed confession in the cookie jar? As it turned out I found nothing more exciting than a stash of Celestial Seasonings herbal tea.

"Here you go," I said, handing her a steaming mug. "Do you take anything in it?"

"No." She sipped it contentedly. "This is perfect."

I usually take my tea with sugar and Oreos, but having found neither, I settled for drinking it au naturel.

"So," she said, "you're really investigating the murder for Dorcas?"

I nodded. "The police are convinced she killed Vic, but I think she's innocent."

"Poor Dorcas. Vic was so cruel to her."

She sighed deeply.

"I know you must be wondering what I saw in him. Everybody did."

No surprise there.

"It's true Vic had a mean side, but he could be wonderful when he wanted to be. When you felt his love shining on you, you never wanted to get out from under his warmth."

She wrapped her hands around her mug, as if trying to recapture some of that warmth.

"I suspected all along that he was cheating on me, but I wouldn't let myself believe it. After last night, of course, I had to face the truth.

"Look what I found in Vic's suitcase. The one he was packing when the murderer showed up." She picked up a small black appointment book from the coffee table and tossed it to me. "I guess it must be some sort of sex journal."

I opened it and saw a roster of women, listed only by their first names. Next to each name was a one-to-ten ranking, and a brief description of the woman's sexual specialty.

Regan was the most recent entry.

"I'm an eight and a half," Allison said, "and Regan's only an eight. I guess Vic didn't mind, not if she could get him a network deal. For a network deal, he'd probably sleep with a five."

Was she kidding? For a network deal, he'd sleep with his grandmother.

"But neither of us is as good as Holly. She's a nine."

"Holly?"

"The barmaid at the Laff Palace. You remember her. *Cute, but Psycho*?"

Oh. So that's what Pebbles' name was.

I checked her out in the little black book. And sure enough, Holly was a nine. With a star. I blushed when I read her sexual specialty, a practice illegal in at least fourteen states.

Allison shook her curls, bewildered. "I can't believe it. He was cheating on me with Regan and Holly. And all these other women."

Tears welled up in her eyes. "Oh, dear. I can't start crying again. I just can't."

She wiped away the burgeoning tears and turned to me.

"So how can I help you?"

"I think Dorcas was framed. I think somebody stole a pair of pantyhose from her tote bag while she was attacking Vic and used them to strangle him later that night. Did you happen to see anyone go near the bag during the attack?"

"I don't think anybody was looking at the bag. We were all looking at Dorcas."

"That's what the killer was counting on."

"You really think Dorcas is innocent?"

"Yes," I said. And then, on a hunch, I added: "Don't you?"

She took a thoughtful sip of her tea.

"I do," she said finally. "I know she hated Vic, but I doubt she's a killer. To be perfectly honest, there was a part of me that wanted to jump on Vic and attack him myself." She smiled wryly. "Maybe she just beat me to the punch."

I couldn't picture Allison, with her cabbage roses and pink pajamas, jumping anyone, let alone strangling them. Nevertheless I had to check her alibi. It's Lesson Number One in private eye school. Not that I've ever been to private eye school. But I'm sure it must be Lesson Number One.

"This is awkward," I said, "but do you mind my asking where you were the night of the murder?"

"No, I don't mind. I spent the night at Hank's place."

"Oh?"

"It's not what you think," she hastened to assure me. "He gave me his bed and he slept on the sofa. It was strictly platonic."

Maybe it was platonic on her part, but I remembered the longing in Hank's eyes when he was comforting Allison at the club. I'd bet my bottom Pop-Tart Hank's feelings for her were far from platonic.

The violin concerto came to an end, and so apparently had our interview.

"I'm sorry," Allison said. "I can't talk anymore. I need to rest."

"Of course," I said, getting up. "One last thing, though. Do you mind giving me Hank's address? I'd like to talk with him and see if he remembers seeing anyone near Dorcas's bag."

She gave me the address, then walked me to the door. When she opened it, the sun shone in, glinting off her auburn curls.

"You know," she said, her eyes misting with tears, "in spite of everything that's happened, there's a part of me that still loves Vic."

My God, that was just what Dorcas had said. What sort of spell had Vic cast over these women?

The sooner I could break that spell, the better.

"Did you know," I said, "that Dorcas was once married to Vic?"

Her eyes widened in disbelief.

"You can't be serious."

I nodded. "Dead serious."

"Omigod," she said, stunned. "The poor thing. How could Vic have been so cruel to her?"

For the first time, I saw a look of disgust in her eyes.

I thanked her for her time and headed down to the picket fence, feeling quite pleased with myself. If I'd shortened her mourning period by even one minute, I'd done my good deed for the day.

I spent the next hour or so questioning Allison's neighbors, hoping one of them saw somebody other than Dorcas show up at the bungalow the night of the murder. But nobody saw anything, except the neighbor across the street—the one who called the cops.

A harried young mother with sleep-deprived eyes, she answered the door with an infant slung over her shoulder and a little boy in a Batman suit clinging to her jeans. Her T-shirt was splotched with what looked like dried oatmeal. (At least I hoped it was oatmeal.) And I thought I could see a few flecks of the stuff in her hair, too.

Somebody was having a rough morning.

"You with the police?" she asked when I told her I was investigating Vic's murder.

"No, private eye," I said, flashing her my library card before she could get a good look at it.

I don't know what it is about laminated cards, but they tend to make people take you seriously. Any inhibitions she had about talking to a stranger disappeared.

"Like I told the police, all I saw was a tall, skinny girl banging on the door, drunk as a skunk. She woke up the baby. At four A.M! It took me hours to get her back down again." She raked her fingers through her oatmeal-encrusted hair. "Dwayne, stop pulling at Mommy's jeans."

The little boy stopped tugging at her jeans and threw his arms around her thigh instead.

"Dwayne, you're cutting off my circulation."

"I woke up, too," he informed me solemnly.

I smiled at him and turned back to his mom. "Are you certain you didn't see anybody else show up that night?"

"No, nobody else. Just the drunk."

"I saw Batman!" Dwayne released his death grip on his mother's thigh. "In his Batmobile!"

He whirled around in his Batman cape, for dramatic effect.

"I saw Batman!" he repeated, in case I hadn't caught it the first time. "In his Batmobile."

"He's seen *Batman*, all right," his mom said. "About 67 times. We bought the video. Worst mistake we ever made. If I hear that theme song one more time, I may hurl myself off a cliff."

All traces of shyness vanished, Dwayne was now spinning around in a frenzy, yelling, "I saw Batman! I saw Batman!"

No doubt thrilled that her older brother had spotted a world-famous action hero, the baby joined in the fun and began wailing at the top of her lungs.

Their mother groaned.

"Sorry, gotta go."

And she shut the door not so gently in my face.

As I made my way back to Wheezy, I could still hear Dwayne shrieking, "I saw Batman! I saw Batman!"

Great. Another expert eyewitness joins the Jaine Austen investigative team.

After a quick pit stop at McDonald's for a restorative Quarter Pounder, I headed over to pay a call on Vic's writer, Hank.

As those of you paying attention may recall, Dorcas wasn't the only one who'd attacked Vic at the Laff Palace. Hank had lunged at him, too, furious at the way he'd so callously dumped

Allison. True, Vic had brushed him aside like a pesky gnat. But who's to say Hank didn't show up at the bungalow later that night and have better luck with a pair of pantyhose?

It was a short hop to Hank's place in Culver City, one of those spit and cardboard singles buildings that seem to spring up overnight like weeds in L.A.

Hank opened the door to his apartment in shorts and a sweatshirt. Without his jeans and blazer, he was skinny as a runway model, with a waist I'd kill for and knees as knobby as golf balls.

Not exactly the portrait of an assassin.

"Hi," I said. "I'm Jaine Austen."

"Love your books."

I forced a smile, as if I hadn't heard that one a gazillion times.

"Actually," I started to explain, "I'm investigating Vic's murder."

"I know. Allison called and told me you'd be stopping by."

He ushered me into his apartment, a no-frills bachelor pad decorated with mismatched furniture and Laurel & Hardy movie posters. The only expensive object in the room was a fancy exercise machine, draped with clothing.

"I spent hundreds of dollars on that damn machine," he said, following my gaze, "and used it maybe three times. Now it's a coat rack."

"I can relate," I said, thinking of all the gym memberships I'd let lapse in my lifetime. "Anyhow, I really appreciate your talking with me."

"No problem. I was just about to take a break." He pointed to a laptop computer on a card table in the far corner of the room. "Like everybody else in town," he grinned, "I'm writing a movie."

And he was not exaggerating. Nine out of ten Angelinos are writing movies. (The tenth is writing a sitcom.)

"You want a Coke?" he asked.

"Sure."

He walked past the counter separating his tiny dining area from his tiny kitchen and got us two Cokes from the refrigerator.

"Grab a seat," he called out to me.

I sat down at his dinette set and watched him struggle to open the pop-tops on the Cokes. Not exactly Mr. Universe, was he? No wonder he'd backed down from his confrontation with Vic at the Laff Palace.

"Anyhow," he said, coming back with the Cokes, "the answer is no."

I blinked, puzzled.

"Allison told me you'd be asking me if I saw anybody go near Dorcas's bag the night of the murder. Well, I didn't. Just thought I'd save you some time. I didn't see anybody lift a pair of pantyhose from her bag."

"Even if you didn't see anyone, can you think of anyone, other than Dorcas, who might've killed Vic?"

"Take a number. Everybody hated the guy."

"Did you?"

Of course, I already knew the answer to that one.

"Sure. You saw the way I told him off at the club. He treated me like crap. But what I really hated was the way he treated Allison. The creep was ready to hop into bed with anyone without a Y chromosome."

Hank had hated Vic, all right. Enough, I wondered, to have summoned up the strength to kill him?

"Allison says she slept here that night."

"She did. So in case you're thinking she killed Vic, forget it. She was here all night and I'm prepared to swear to it."

"She said you slept in the living room and she slept in the bedroom."

"That's true."

"How do you know she didn't sneak out in the middle of the night while you were sleeping?"

"I'm a light sleeper. I would've heard her."

I wasn't so sure about that. I was convinced Hank would perjure himself up his yingyang to save his beloved. Either one of them could've slipped out past the other in the middle of the night and killed Vic.

"And I didn't do it, either," he said, "if that's what you're wondering. I hated the guy, but I didn't kill him."

And I believed him. Hank couldn't open a pop-top without a struggle, let alone wring the life out of someone.

Besides, I thought as I got up to leave, anybody who used an exercise machine as a coat rack was A-OK in my book.

Chapter 11

It was a little before three when I left Hank's place. Which gave me just enough time to zip over to Santa Monica for my appointment at Gustavo's. (That is, if you call crawling along in Wheezy at twenty-five miles an hour "zipping.")

The salon was on Montana Avenue, one of the toniest streets in Santa Monica, or as I like to think of it, Big-Bucks-By-The-Sea.

A valet parker stood out front, but I'd be darned if I'd spend money I didn't have for a valet. So I parked three long blocks away on a residential street and sprinted back to the salon.

It wasn't until I got there and saw my reflection in Gustavo's plate glass window that I realized I was wearing my usual elastic-waist jeans and T-shirt ensemble. I looked around at the toney Montana Avenue crowd. Not an elastic waist in sight. And all the T-shirts were the tight spandex midriff-exposing kind, not the big baggy Hanes Men's Underwear kind.

Drat. Why hadn't I planned ahead and worn something decent? Oh, well. It was too late to do anything about it now. I took a deep breath, sucked in my gut, and headed inside.

The place was a haven of pale peach walls and recessed

lighting guaranteed to shave years off a woman's face. Soft music played in the background as pretty ladies lounged around getting prettier.

I'd worried that Gustavo's would be full of avant garde stylists with purple hair and nostril rings, but to my relief the staff sported impeccable cuts and no discernible facial jewelry.

I walked up to a doll-like brunette at the reception desk. She looked up at me with enormous blue eyes, which lingered on my T-shirt. I glanced down and cringed to see a large ketchup stain, a souvenir, no doubt, from my Quarter Pounder.

"Deliveries around the back," she said.

"Actually, I'm here for an appointment with Gustavo. I'm Jaine Austen."

She jumped up from her chair, oozing apologies.

"I'm so sorry, Ms. Austen. I had no idea! I'm Deedee. Come right this way, and we'll get you into a styling robe."

Well, that was good news. The sooner I got out of my wrong-side-of-the-tracks outfit, the better.

I followed her to the rear of the salon, trying to ignore the curious glances I was attracting. Needless to say, I did not fit Gustavo's typical demographic.

Deedee showed me to a softly lit dressing room, where I changed into a black wraparound smock and matching scuff slippers.

"They're for your pedicure," Deedee explained, when I asked about the slippers.

"I'm getting a pedicure, too?"

"You're getting the works," she said, with a wide smile, and led me to Gustavo's station.

All the other stylists worked out in the open, but Gustavo

had a private sanctuary, shut off from the rest of the salon by silk moire curtains.

Deedee deposited me in a plush leather salon chair.

"Gustavo will be right with you. Can I get you anything while you're waiting? A latte?"

"That sounds great."

"How about a warm croissant with homemade raspberry preserves?"

Absolutely not. No croissants. Not after that Quarter Pounder. Not if I wanted to look good for my date with Andrew.

"Sure. Why not?"

(You didn't really think I was going to say no, did you?)

Seconds later she brought me my latte and croissant, which I managed to polish off just as Gustavo came sailing into the room.

Tall and dark, with a long shiny ponytail, he wore skin-tight black jeans and a spandex top. I could see every muscle in his six-pack abs.

"Ms. Austen," he said, kissing my hand. (I only hoped it didn't smell of onions from my Quarter Pounder.) "What a pleasure to meet you! I love your work!"

I had no idea who he thought I was, but whoever it was had to be somebody important. For a fleeting instant I wondered if he thought I was the real Jane Austen. Was it possible he didn't realize she'd been dead and buried for nearly 200 years?

"Let me take a good look at you."

He began circling the chair, eyeing my hair much like I imagine Michelangelo checked out the ceiling of the Sistine Chapel.

"You've got awesome hair. You know that, don't you?"

"But it's so curly," I moaned.

"That's why it's great. Curls are in."

"Actually, I was hoping you could straighten it out."

"Oh, no!" He looked horrified." It would be criminal to straighten this fabulous hair. I think we should go with a cloud of soft curls. The Kate Winslet *Titanic* look."

"It won't be frizzy?" I asked.

"Oh, no. Just soft, beautiful curls. And let's add some auburn highlights."

I swallowed, hesitant. I'd been hoping for sleek, shiny straight hair, the kind of straight hair I can get only at a hair salon.

"Trust me," he said. "You're going to look spectacular."

Then I thought of all the ladies I saw out in the salon and how wonderful they looked.

"Okay," I said, "let's do it."

"Sabrosa!"

He snapped his fingers and a trio of assistants materialized, one of them wheeling in preparations for Gustavo to highlight my hair.

"Usually I let the colorist do it," he said, "but for my special customers, I like to do it myself." Accent on the *special*.

If he only knew the truth, that he was slaving over the woman who wrote—not *Pride & Prejudice*—but *We Clean for You. We Press for You. We Even Dye for You.*

He proceeded to dab on my highlights with painstaking care, barking orders to his assistants, who hovered nearby, handing him foil wraps on demand.

While waiting for the color to set, I was transferred to an overstuffed chaise, where I was plied with more croissants and treated to a pedicure by a darling slip of a thing named Ron.

Ron went right to work, trimming and pumicing and polishing up a storm.

"Voila!" he said when he was through. "Behold."

I blinked in amazement. Never had my toes looked so good. He'd painted my nails a beautiful creamy peach, and shaped them to perfection. Really, if the bottom ever fell out of the writing biz, I could be a toe model.

Next I was whisked to Kyra, the shampoo girl, who gave me what had to be the most relaxing shampoo of my life. Whatever shampoo she was using smelled divine. Like night-blooming jasmine.

I sat back as Kyra massaged my scalp with magic fingers. The last time I felt that relaxed, I'd been hanging out with my good buddy Jose Cuervo. All too soon, she slathered me with crème rinse and the shampoo came to an end.

"Wow, you look awesome," she said, as she surveyed my new color. "Amazing!"

"Let me see."

"No, not yet. Gustavo likes his customers to wait until he's all done to see the final results. It's much more dramatic that way." She grinned. "Don't worry, you're gonna love it."

A fluffy towel wrapped around my head, I was led back to Gustavo's sanctuary, where he sat me down facing away from the mirror and, with fierce concentration, began cutting my hair.

I wished I could watch what he was doing, but with all his minions hovering about it would've been impossible to see the mirror, anyway.

Finally, after much squinting and humming of "Besame Mucho," my cut was finished.

"Dryer!" Gustavo shrieked.

One of the assistants held a dryer as Gustavo alternately fluffed and scrunched my hair. As he worked, his minions exploded with oohs and aahs of approval. By now, I was really excited. If my hair was anything like my toes, I'd be stunning.

Finally he was finished.

"It's perfect," he said, nodding solemnly. "Just what I was going for."

All the minions chimed in with a congratulatory round of "perfects" and "awesomes" and "amazings."

"Ready to look?" he asked.

I nodded, feeling like a contestant on *Extreme Make-over*.

With a dramatic flourish he swiveled my chair around to face the mirror. But one of his assistants was standing in the way, a woman I hadn't noticed before, a gal with a ghastly mess of frizzy red hair.

I was just about to ask her if she'd mind stepping aside when it dawned on me that nobody was standing in my way. That was *my* reflection in the mirror. The woman with the ghastly red frizz was *me*!

Suddenly I felt sick to my stomach. The auburn highlights Gustavo promised me were a Sunkist orange. And the "soft" curls were straight out of a Brillo box.

"So what do you think?" Gustavo beamed with pride.

"It's not exactly what I expected," I gulped.

His smile froze.

"Oh?" Icicles dripped from the syllable. "And what, may I ask, is wrong?"

Nothing, if you don't mind looking like Ronald McDonald on estrogen.

"Um, the color's a little bright."

"The color's awesome." He turned to his minions. "What do you think, people? Do you like the color?"

A fawning chorus of "awesomes" filled the air.

"Well, if you'll excuse me," Gustavo said, making a big show of checking his watch, "I've got other clients waiting."

He gestured for me to get out of the chair.

I couldn't let this happen. I had to say something. But what? I couldn't ask for my money back. I hadn't paid anything.

"Well?" he said, waiting for me to get up from the chair.

I had to stand up for my rights and tell him I wasn't going anywhere until he fixed my hair and made me look like a member of the human race again.

It wasn't easy, but I gathered my courage and spoke up.

"I'm sorry," I said, "but I simply can't leave without—"

"Without what?" He shot me a withering glare.

"Without asking where you get your croissants. They're awesome."

Okay, so I'm a sniveling weakling, a disgrace to assertive women everywhere. What can I say? You'd snivel, too, if you were surrounded by a bunch of beautiful people looking down their nose jobs at you.

I slunk out of the salon and trudged back to my car, wondering if Andrew would notice if I wore a paper bag over my head on our date that night.

Oh, well. At least my toes looked good.

And besides, it was only a little after five. Andrew said he'd pick me up at 7:30. If I stopped at the drugstore for some hair color, maybe I could color my hair and blow it dry before he showed up. I raced to Wheezy, only to find a $60 parking ticket plastered on the windshield. I'd exceeded the two-hour parking limit by ten measly minutes. Arggh!

I got in the car and caught a glimpse of myself in the rearview mirror. I would've burst into tears, but I didn't have time to cry. Instead, I chugged over to the nearest drugstore and grabbed a bottle of hair color called Tawny Breeze, a pretty chestnut brown, light years nicer than the Orange Hurricane I was currently sporting.

Just my luck, when I got to the front of the store to pay for it, there was only one lone clerk and about a gazillion customers. I got on line and waited for what seemed like decades, while my fellow shoppers amused themselves by whispering about my hair.

Finally I made it up to the clerk, a brittle, gum-chewing woman who, as I was about to learn, had clearly been napping the day they taught Tact 101.

I handed her the Tawny Breeze.

"Not a moment too soon, honey," she said, eyeing my neon mop. "Not a moment too soon."

Ignoring the giggles of my fellow shoppers, I raced back out to the car and checked the time. Twenty to six. If I could make it home in twenty minutes, I still might have a shot at fixing my hair.

I strapped myself in Wheezy and floored it all the way home. Which—in Wheezy-speak—means I was doing thirty miles an hour.

I pulled up in front of my duplex a few minutes past six. I grabbed my Tawny Breeze and was dashing up the path to my apartment when suddenly I froze in my tracks.

There, sitting on my front step, was Andrew. What the heck was he doing here so early?

I couldn't possibly let him see me this way. I'd just have to duck behind my neighbor's azalea bush and hide there for the rest of my life, if need be.

But it was too late. He'd already seen me.

"Hi, Jaine!" he said, waving.

Oh, Lord. What was I going to do now? Maybe I could

pretend I wasn't me, that I was my much less attractive twin sister.

"I got through work early," he said, "so I decided to stop by. Is that okay?"

"Sure." I smiled weakly.

I only hoped he was a toe man.

Chapter 12

"What the heck happened to your hair?" Andrew said when I let him into the apartment.

Okay, his exact words were, "Nice place you've got here," but I knew that's what he was thinking as he eyed my Day-Glo tresses.

"And what a great cat!"

I looked down and saw Prozac at Andrew's feet, staring up at him. Here he was, at last. Her archenemy. The invader. The rival for my affections.

"She's not good with strangers," I warned.

I was about to snatch her away before she could claw his eyes out when, to my amazement, she began rubbing her body against his ankles, purring as loud as a buzz saw.

She looked over at me, her eyes slitted in ecstasy.

You never told me he was so cute.

Can you believe that cat? For days she'd been in a full-tilt snit over my date with Andrew, and now here she was throwing herself at him. What a shameless hussy!

"Now, Prozac," I said. "Don't bother Andrew."

"Oh, she's no bother. I love cats."

He picked her up and began stroking her fur with slow, rhythmic motions.

Some cats have all the luck.

"If you'll excuse me," I said, "I'd better go change. Can I get you anything while you're waiting? Some wine, maybe? A Coke?"

"No, I'm good."

Prozac purred like a starlet in an X-rated video.

Me, too.

I left the two of them going at it hot and heavy on the sofa and went to the bedroom to change. I tossed on a pair of black crepe slacks (with a Lance-approved set-in waistband) and a black cashmere turtleneck, then surveyed myself in the mirror. With my orange hair and black outfit, I could rent myself out as a Halloween costume.

Luckily, Gustavo had left my hair long enough for a ponytail. I somehow managed to corral my mountain of curls into a scrunchy. Which, I was heartened to see, was a bit of an improvement. And, as I noticed when I checked myself out in the mirror again, the black outfit was actually kind of slimming. So maybe I didn't look so horrendous after all.

For the first time since I came home, I was beginning to feel a glimmer of hope. A glimmer that was quickly dashed to smithereens when I returned to the living room. Prozac had left the heavenly confines of Andrew's lap and was prancing around with something gray and dingy dangling from her mouth.

"Now, Prozac," I chided. "Andrew doesn't want to play with your rubber mouse."

But as I was about to learn when she dropped her little gift at Andrew's feet, it wasn't her rubber mouse. Or her catnip kitty.

"What's this?" Andrew said, picking it up.

Yikes! It was a pair of my ratty old underpants, the ones I use as a dust rag. She must've dug them out from the broom closet.

Prozac was practically doing a jig at Andrew's feet, she was so damn proud of herself.

They're hilarious, huh? I thought you'd get a kick out of them.

"Oh, Prozac," I said, grabbing my panties from Andrew's hands. "You naughty girl, rummaging in the neighbor's trash again."

Yeah, right. Like he's really going to believe that.

Some day, I swear, I'm going to put that cat up for adoption.

My mind was a blur on the drive over to the restaurant. All I could think of was Prozac prancing around the living room with my panties in her mouth. As Andrew chatted about life in Germany, I barely managed to respond with a few carefully placed *Um, how interesting*'s.

But it didn't matter. Nothing mattered anymore. By now I was convinced that my date with Andrew was destined for the fiasco file. I dreaded to think what further humiliations awaited me before the night was over. Would I spend the entire evening with a hunk of spinach permanently welded to my front tooth?

But the fates, those pesky devils, surprised me.

The restaurant turned out to be a charming candlelit spot out by the beach. (Not that we needed a candle; we could read our menus by the glow of my hair.)

I don't know if it was our cozy table for two. Or the waves crashing beneath our feet. Or the mellow Frank Sinatra love songs playing in the background. Probably it was the glass of white wine I practically inhaled the minute the waiter gave it to me. All I know is that a half hour later, things were looking a whole lot rosier.

"I suppose you're wondering about my hair," I said, figuring I might as well get it out in the open instead of trying to pretend I wasn't sitting there like the reincarnation of Little Orphan Annie.

"No," Andrew lied. "Not at all."

"Oh, come on," I said, reaching for a piece of deliciously crusty sourdough bread.

"I look like a pumpkin just gave birth on my head."

"So what happened?" he said, trying to keep a straight face.

"I got ambushed by a psychotic stylist."

"It's really not that bad. And besides," he added, with a sexy smile, "I happen to think pumpkins are delicious."

Oh, my, yes. Things were definitely looking rosier.

Our waiter, a laid-back dude who looked like he just came in off his surfboard, gave us menus.

"They've got a whole section of low-fat dishes," Andrew said. "Everything cooked with natural ingredients and no cholesterol."

Oh, foo. That sure didn't sound like fun.

Then he grinned.

"I never order from that section. I always get the New York strip steak and baked potato. It's to die for."

We both ordered the steak, and Andrew poured me some more wine.

"So tell me about yourself," he said.

"You already know a lot about me. After all, you've read my resume."

"True, but I'm sure there's life after Toiletmasters."

Little did he know.

I put on my First Date tap shoes and told him how I liked to read and do crossword puzzles and work out at the gym and go to the movies and eat Ben & Jerry's in bed.

Okay, so I lied about working out and left out the part about eating Ben & Jerry's in bed.

"You ever been married?" he asked.

"Yes, once, but it didn't work out."

No sense ruining his appetite with the gruesome details.

"How about you?" I asked. "Ever tie the knot?"

"No, but I've been on the brink."

I thought how lovely it would be to be on the brink with Andrew.

Dinner came, and it was, as advertised, to die for.

And so was Andrew. On the drive over, I had visions of us sitting across from each other with absolutely nothing to say, Andrew filling the gaping holes in our conversation with stuffy banker chat about IPOs and GNPs and SECs, the kind of chat that tends to make me doze off into my soup.

But I'm happy to report that Andrew was amazingly easy to talk to. We talked about everything—our childhoods, our parents, the universal nightmare known as high school, and our favorite books and movies and TV shows. (His, in case you're interested, were *Catcher in the Rye, Tootsie,* and *Alf.*)

As it turned out I, too, was an *Alf* aficionado and we spent at least ten minutes testing each other on *Alf* trivia.

"Where did Alf go to high school?"

"Melmac High!"

"How old was he?"

"229!"

"What sport did he participate in?"

"Captain of the Bouillabaisseball team!"

"Wow," Andrew said after I scored with the bouillabaisseball answer. "You're good."

I beamed with pride, all those hours glued to the TV when I should've been doing my homework having finally paid off.

Before I knew it, we'd plowed our way through our steaks and baked potatoes and a heavenly chocolate mousse for dessert. My waistband was a tad tight, and frankly, so was I.

"How about a walk on the beach," Andrew suggested, "to burn off some calories?"

Of course, I would've had to walk to Fresno and back to burn off the calories I'd packed away, but the thought of a walk on the beach with Andrew sounded terrific.

"Sure," I said, "let's do it."

And so we clambered down a steep incline onto the beach, took off our shoes, and began walking along the shore, our bare feet squishing in the sand. And for once I didn't have to worry about my hair frizzing in the damp. Thanks to Gustavo, it couldn't possibly get any frizzier.

We walked for a while, burning off calories, sucking in the marvelous sea air.

Then suddenly Andrew stopped and stared out at the ocean, its whitecaps glittering in the moonlight.

"Isn't it fantastic?" he sighed.

"Yes," I echoed, looking not at the whitecaps but at Andrew's profile in the moonlight. "Fantastic."

We stood there under a silvery moon, the waves breaking at our feet, like Burt Lancaster and Deborah Kerr in *From Here to Eternity*. I almost expected to hear the swell of violins and crash of cymbals in the background. If that wasn't the perfect setting for Andrew to take me in his arms and kiss me, I don't know what was.

But sad to say, he just turned to me and said, "Ready to go?"

"Sure," I said, hiding my disappointment with a feeble smile.

As we headed back up to the parking lot, I was flooded with doubts. What if he wasn't really interested in me? What if he'd just been polite all night? After all, if he really liked me, wouldn't he have tried to kiss me?

By the time we pulled up in front of my duplex, I was convinced the spark I'd seen in his eyes at the dinner table was just the glare from my hair.

"Well, thanks for a lovely evening," I said stiffly.

"Thank *you*. I had a great time."

Then he smiled as if he meant it. And I wondered if maybe he *was* interested, after all.

"Would you like to come in for some coffee," I asked, "or an after-dinner drink?"

"An after-dinner drink sounds great."

As it turned out, the only after-dinner drinks I had were Nestle's Quik and Campbell's Chicken Noodle Soup.

"Gee," I said, searching the linen closet I call my liquor cabinet, "I could've sworn I had some Grand Marnier in here somewhere."

"That's okay," Andrew said from where he was sitting on the sofa. "I didn't really want a drink. I just didn't want the evening to end."

"Oh?" My voice came out in a tiny squeak.

"Yes, I thought we could talk some more."

He patted the cushion next to him, beckoning me to join him.

I sucked in my gut and walked over to the sofa, then sat down next to him, my heart pounding.

It didn't look like Andrew was about to do any talking. Instead, he reached over and touched my cheek. With that touch I felt stirrings I hadn't felt in a long time. I felt warm and melty; I felt ripe and ready—

Oh, damn. I felt Prozac's furry body worming her way between us.

"Well, look who's here!" Andrew grinned, pulling her up into his lap.

Hi, handsome!

She rolled over for a belly rub.

I'm all yours, big boy.

Wait a minute! I felt like shouting. *That's my line!*

He rubbed her belly and she purred in ecstasy.

I smiled stiffly, wondering if I should demand my money back from the doctor who supposedly spayed her.

"I think somebody around here needs to go potty," I said, shooting her a dirty look.

Fine with me. Don't hurry back.

"Jaine's right," Andrew said, putting her back down. "Be a good girl and go potty."

Anything you say, lover.

And you won't believe this (I still don't), but she actually wandered off to her litter box! This from a cat who hadn't obeyed a single order from the moment I adopted her.

"Now where were we?" Andrew said, once again touching my cheek.

Another jolt of excitement coursed through my body, and before I knew it, he was leaning in to kiss me.

Here it was: The moment I'd been waiting for ever since the day I first laid eyes on him. I was so excited I could hardly breathe. I only hoped I wouldn't pop a button on my waistband and knock his eye out.

Our lips were just about to touch when his cell phone rang. Damndamndamndamndamn!

Don't let him answer it, I prayed. *Don't let him answer it.*

But once again the fates were about to desert me.

He shrugged apologetically and opened his phone.

"Yes . . I see. . . . Okay, I'll be right there." He flipped his phone shut. "That was Sam. Emergency down at the bank."

"At ten o'clock on a Saturday night?"

"She stayed late to work on our project. She's having trouble with the computer, and she needs me.

"Sorry," he sighed, "but I've really got to go."

"Oh, sure." I plastered a phony smile on my face. "I understand."

He kissed me lightly on the forehead. Not exactly the suctionfest I'd been hoping for. Clearly the phone call from Sam had broken the spell. I couldn't help wondering if he still felt something for her, after all.

"I'll call you soon."

"Right. Sure."

I stood at the doorway as he hurried down the path to his car.

Computer troubles, my fanny, I thought as I watched his retreating figure. The bitch just wanted to keep us apart.

YOU'VE GOT MAIL!

TAMPA TRIBUNE

Daring Shirt Theft

Movie patrons at the Tampa Megaplex 15 were stunned yesterday when a deranged moviegoer accosted a man on the ticket line and stole the shirt right off his back.

The shirt in question was a silk Hawaiian sports shirt, and the victim was Herman Kotler, 69, of Clearwater.

"I was standing on line minding my own business," the shaken Kotler said, "when suddenly this crazy man came up to me and insisted that I was wearing his shirt. He kept talking about a 'lucky gravy stain.' The guy was nuts! I bought that shirt 15 years ago in Hawaii. The next thing I knew, he ripped it off me, and took off down the street, dragging his wife behind him."

"For an old geezer, he sure could run," said moviegoer Eduardo Solis, 42, who chased the shirt thief for three blocks.

Witnesses with information about the identity of the assailant are requested to contact Det. John Vincenzo of the Tampa Police Department, (813) 555-6874.

To: Jausten
From: Shoptillyoudrop
Subject: Your Daddy, the Shirt Thief

Jaine, honey, you won't believe what happened at the movies. It was horrible. Just horrible!

Daddy and I went to see the 3:20 show of that adorable new Sarah Jessica Paltrow movie, but somehow Daddy got the time wrong, and when we got there the movie had already started, so we decided to get tickets for the new Harvey Porter movie instead, which was so disappointing as I'd really been looking forward to seeing Sarah Jessica Paltrow; I just loved her in *Friends*. But that's not the horrible news, darling. I'm afraid I got a bit sidetracked. Daddy says I'm always doing that, that I can never get to the point of a story, but Daddy's got a lot of nerve criticizing me after what he just put me through.

Anyhow, here's what happened. We were standing on line when suddenly Daddy gasped and said, "Do you see what I see?" And I said, "Oh my gosh, yes! They've gone and raised the ticket prices another dollar!" And Daddy said, "Not that. Look at that man over there. He's wearing my shirt!"

And sure enough, there was a man on line ahead of us in an orange Hawaiian shirt that looked an awful lot like Daddy's. Well, before I could stop him, Daddy ran over to the fellow.

"Excuse me, sir," he said, "I believe you're wearing my shirt." The man said it wasn't Daddy's shirt, that he bought it fifteen years ago in Hawaii, but Daddy refused to believe him. He swore he saw his "lucky gravy stain" on the lapel. The man said it wasn't a gravy stain but a minestrone stain, and Daddy accused the man of being a bald-faced liar.

By now everybody on line was staring at us, and I was sorry I ever suggested going to the movies in the first place. Then suddenly, before my horrified eyes, Daddy ripped the shirt right off the poor man's back! In broad daylight! Like a common criminal on *CSI: Tampa Vistas*!

Then Daddy grabbed me by the arm, and we took off down the street to our car, which was parked six blocks away, because Daddy couldn't find a parking space and refused to pay money to park in the lot. I haven't run so fast since high school gym class. I'm surprised I didn't wind up with a heart attack!

No doubt about it. Your daddy has lost his mind.

Your miserable,
Mom

P.S. Now every time the doorbell rings, I think it's the police come to arrest Daddy. The way I'm feeling right now, I'm not sure I'd mind.

To: Jausten
From: DaddyO
Subject: Great News!

Great news, lambchop! I got my lucky shirt back!

I suppose Mom e-mailed you the newspaper story. It just goes to show you can't believe everything you read in the paper. That Kotler guy was lying through his teeth. He was wearing my lucky shirt, all right. I knew it the minute I saw it. I tried to be reasonable with him, but he wouldn't listen. So I had no other choice but to grab it and run like a bat out of hell.

I'm seriously thinking of suing the paper for calling me a "shirt thief." Not to mention the clown who called me an old geezer.

Mom is afraid the cops are going to arrest me. Nonsense. They'll never track me down. And if they do, so what? I only took what was rightfully mine!

Of course, Mom is a bit miffed with me for dragging her six blocks in her flip-flops. But the important thing is, I've got my shirt back—and my good luck! Today I beat Ed Peters at miniature golf and found a parking spot right outside Ye Olde Fudge Shoppe. (Don't tell Mom; she thinks I kicked my fudge habit years ago.)

Lots of love from your lucky,
Daddy

Chapter 13

I spent a restless night dreaming of Andrew and Sam making love over a hot spreadsheet while I stood by trapped in a vat of pureed pumpkins.

What a nightmare. But not quite as bad as the nightmare that awaited me the next morning when I looked in the mirror and saw my hair in the cruel light of day. I didn't think it was possible, but it looked even worse than it had yesterday. Somehow, overnight, it had gone from merely disgustingly bright to a pulsating, eyeball-peeling neon. I practically needed sunglasses to brush my teeth.

No doubt about it. First thing after breakfast, I was going to color my hair.

"I shouldn't be feeding you," I said to Prozac as she yowled at my ankles for her breakfast. "Not after that vile panty gag you pulled last night."

Oh, come on. It was hysterical.

It was with a distinctly cold shoulder that I tossed her some Luscious Lamb Guts.

Oblivious to my snub, she buried her nose in the stuff, sucking it up with orgiastic abandon. I left her going at it and nuked a couple of frozen waffles for myself. Too bad I was all out of syrup. Oh, well. I'd just have to use peanut butter.

I settled down at the computer with my gourmet breakfast and checked my e-mails. I knew I shouldn't open the letters from my parents, not if I wanted to enjoy my breakfast. But curiosity got the better of me, and I read all about Daddy's new career as a shirt thief. I only hoped Mom—in a desperate attempt to clean out Daddy's closets for good—wouldn't rat on Daddy to the cops.

I polished off my waffles, trying not to think of Daddy behind bars in his "lucky" Hawaiian shirt, and was just about to head off to the bathroom to dye my hair when the doorbell rang.

It was Lance, dressed for work in one of his impeccably tailored suits.

"Oh, my God!" he gasped when I opened the door. "Who colored your hair? Sherwin Williams?"

"Thanks, and good morning to you, too."

"What monster did this to you?" he asked, running his fingers through my frizz.

"Gustavo."

"Gustavo Mendes? The A-list Gustavo? The one everybody's raving about? That Gustavo?"

"None other."

"I don't believe it."

"I didn't either."

"Well, you can't possibly live with it this way."

"I know. I was just about to color it."

I showed him my bottle of Tawny Breeze.

"No way," he said, snatching the bottle from my hands. "You're not doing it yourself. You're going back to Gustavo and make him fix it."

"Oh, no I'm not," I said, still burning at the memory of how I'd melted under Gustavo's withering glare. "He happens to be a very intimidating guy."

"He can't intimidate me," Lance said, his blond curls shaking with indignation. "I'll go back with you. I'm not afraid of any 'A-list' hairdresser."

Standing there, his jaw clenched in anger, he looked every inch a designer-clad avenging angel.

"Well, okay," I said. "If you really think it'll work."

"Of course it'll work. The guy won't know what hit him."

We made a date to meet the next day at Gustavo's salon, and Lance hurried off to do battle with the shoe divas at Neiman's.

Having abandoned my plans to color my hair, I settled down on the sofa with the Sunday newspaper. Splashed on the front page of the Calendar section was a story about Vic, one of those death-of-a-rising-star tributes, filled with insincere quotes from Hollywood types eager to get their names in print.

Seeing that story jolted me back to reality. Dorcas may not have been front-page news anymore, but that didn't change the fact that she was still festering away in jail. And I still had no idea who the killer was. I had to stop obsessing about my hair and get back on the case.

So far, none of the suspects I'd visited seemed like encouraging prospects. But what about Pebbles, the jilted lover? I remembered the look of rage on her face when Vic announced his engagement to Regan. I could easily picture her wringing Vic's neck.

Yes, it was time to pay Pebbles a little visit.

I tried getting her number from information but she wasn't listed. I'd have to wait until the Laff Palace opened and talk to her then.

I spent the rest of the day hanging around my apartment waiting in vain for Andrew to call, then shoved my Day-Glo mop in a baseball cap and headed over to the Laff Palace for a little tête-à-tête with *Cute, but Psycho*.

Pebbles was nowhere in sight when I showed up at the club. But Pete the bartender was on duty behind the bar, wiping glasses with his filthy dishrag.

His eyes lit up at the sight of me.

"Hey, doll. How's it going?"

"Er . . . fine, thanks."

"Grab a seat and chat a while. Sundays are always slow. I'll bring you a complimentary tap water."

"I'd better not. I'm driving."

"Haha," he grinned, exposing the gap in his front teeth. "I like a woman with a sense of humor. That was a joke, right?"

"Sort of, yes."

"Say, you look cute in that baseball cap," he said, staring a good two feet below my baseball cap at my boobs.

"I like my women athletic, too," he added, with a wink. "Especially in bed."

Oh, good heavens. Any minute now, I was going to need a barf bag.

"Is Holly here?" I asked.

"Nope. She's off tonight."

"Too bad. I wanted to talk to her."

"About Vic's murder?"

"Yes. How did you know?"

"Spiro told me you were investigating. He says you think Dorcas is innocent."

"I do."

He plucked a maraschino cherry from a none too clean garnish tray and held it out to me. "Want one?"

Not without a tetanus shot.

I shook my head, and he popped it in his mouth.

"So if Dorcas didn't do it," he asked, "who did?"

"For all I know, you did. There certainly wasn't any love lost between you and Vic."

"You're barking up the wrong bartender, doll. Sure, I thought the guy was a jerk, but I didn't wring his neck with a pair of pantyhose."

Then he popped the stem of the cherry in his mouth and ate that, too.

"Speaking of those pantyhose," I said, "did you happen to see anybody go near Dorcas's prop bag that night? Somebody who could've stolen the hose?"

"No," he said, furrowing his caveman brow in concentration, "I don't think so. Frankly, I was distracted."

"By what?"

"By you, sweetcakes. You're hot."

Ugh. Why are the ghastly ones always attracted to me?

"You know, I've always wanted to date a private eye. I have a thing for women in law enforcement."

"Is that so?"

"Yeah. I once dated my parole officer."

Time for a quick change of subject.

"So do you happen to know where Holly lives?"

"Yeah, I happen to know."

"Would you mind telling me?"

"That depends."

"On what?"

"On whether or not you'll go out with me."

"I can't go out with you, Pete. I'm engaged."

"I don't mind. I like a challenge."

"To a woman," I said, using the usually foolproof lesbian rebuff.

"Even better. I also like a threesome."

What did I have to do to get rid of this guy? Tell him I had leprosy?

"Sorry, Pete. I'm just not available."

"Well, if you change your mind . . ."

He took out a greasy business card from his back pocket and handed it to me. It read:

PETE DEL AMO
BARTENDER, BOUNCER AND X-RATED VIDEO SALES

Talk about your renaissance men.

"Call me any time," he leered, "day or night."

File that one under When Hell Freezes Over.

"So can you tell me where Holly lives?" I asked.

"Sure, why not?"

He wrote down Holly's address in a childish scrawl on a cocktail napkin and shot me another one of his gap-toothed grins.

"Now you owe me one, hotcakes."

Oh, yuck. Where the heck was that barf bag?

Holly answered the door to her West Hollywood apartment in shorts and a cropped T-shirt, exposing a washboard tummy and a waist the size of Pete's neck.

"Well, well," she said, tossing her ponytail. "If it isn't the lady writer-detective."

Obviously word traveled fast on the Laff Palace grapevine.

She ushered me in to her living room, a funky affair decorated in what I can only describe as Early Chuck E. Cheese. Her color scheme was an eye-popping hot pink and lime green, with big fuzzy beanbags scattered on the floor. Any minute now, I expected a bunch of five-year-olds to come bursting in for a birthday party.

"Have a seat." She gestured to one of the beanbags.

I scrunched down onto it, wrenching at least five different muscles en route.

"Hope you don't mind if I do my nails while we talk," she said, plopping down on a beanbag across from me. She reached for a jar of nail polish and began polishing her nails a hideous chartreuse.

"By the way," she said, "what happened to your hair? What a disgusting color."

Look who's talking, I wanted to say. *Have you looked at your apartment lately?*

"You ought to sue whoever did that to you for malpractice. You want the name of a good attorney? I know a great guy. Hector Ramirez. He got me five hundred dollars after I developed ingrown hair follicles from a botched bikini wax. I don't remember his number, but he advertises a lot on the back of buses."

"Thanks for the tip." I smiled as if I were grateful, then got down to business. "Do you mind if ask a few questions about the murder?"

"Like what?"

"Like where you were when Vic was killed."

She looked up from her pinky and frowned.

"I don't have to answer that, you know. But I will because I've got nothing to hide. I was home, sleeping."

"Alone?"

"Not that it's any of your business, but yes."

"Not exactly an ironclad alibi."

"What are you saying? That I killed Vic?"

"I don't know. I do know that you had a strong motive."

"Motive? What motive?"

She tried to look like she had no idea what I was talking about.

"Hell hath no fury like a woman scorned."

"Huh?"

"It's a quote from Shakespeare."

"Yeah, well, here's another quote: Screw-eth you."

She went back to painting her nails, applying polish with short angry strokes.

"Look, Peb—I mean, Holly. I heard you talking to Vic outside the supply room. I know you were having an affair with him. I know you expected him to leave Allison for you. And I know you were furious when he dumped both of you for his new agent. If looks could kill, you'd be behind bars now."

She gave me a filthy look (much like the one she'd given Vic) and then started blowing at her nails.

"Okay," she said finally, after she tired of the huffing and puffing bit, "so I was sleeping with the guy. Big deal. So was half of Los Angeles. That doesn't mean I killed him." She stuck her chin out defiantly. "And you can't prove that I did."

She screwed her nail polish shut with a tight twist.

"Now if you don't mind, I've got to get dressed. I've got a date tonight."

So much for mourning Vic.

"Just one more question," I asked, as she hustled me to the door. "Did you happen to see anybody near Dorcas's tote bag the night Vic was killed?"

"As a matter of fact, I did."

"Really?"

My ears perked up. At last, a lead.

"While Dorcas was strangling Vic, I saw Manny bending over her bag."

"Manny? Manny Vernon?"

I remembered Vic's former agent, the rumpled guy with the bad comb-over.

"Are you sure?"

"Yeah, I'm sure. I know what I saw, and I saw Manny bent over that bag."

Chapter 14

Most people think of Hollywood as a glitzy place with a movie star on every corner. Wrong. The real Hollywood is about as glitzy as a cold pizza. And the only people hanging out on street corners charge by the hour.

The Manny Vernon Agency was in the heart of this Hollywood, light-years away from the showbiz power brokers of Beverly Hills.

I tracked down the address on the business card he'd given me, but at first all I saw was a storefront for the Taboo Tattoo Parlor. Then I noticed a small hand-lettered sign in the corner of Taboo's window reading: THE MANNY VERNON AGENCY, 2ND FLOOR.

Hurrying past the yelps of pain coming from the tattoo parlor, I trudged up a termite-eaten flight of stairs. Another hand-lettered sign tacked to one of the doors announced that I was at Manny's office. I knocked on the door, but there was no answer. I poked my head inside and saw a deserted reception area. Its only occupants were an ancient Mr. Coffee machine and a secretary's desk. I surmised from the layers of dust on the desk that there was no actual secretary on duty.

I crossed the reception area to the office beyond.

The door was partially open, and I peeked inside. There I saw Manny Vernon at a battered desk, engrossed in the *TV Guide* crossword puzzle, scratching his comb-over in concentration. His stocky body was crammed into a polyester leisure suit straight out of the *Three's Company* wardrobe department.

Ah, yes. A titan in the showbiz firmament.

"Hello," I said, rapping on the door.

Manny looked up, startled. Clearly, he didn't get many visitors at The Manny Vernon Talent Agency. He battened down his comb-over and quickly stashed the *TV Guide* in a drawer.

"Come in, come in," he said, waving me into the room. "Have a seat."

He gestured to a folding metal chair that looked like it had been around since the dawn of the industrial revolution.

"Let me get you some coffee."

Before I could stop him, he was hustling out to the Mr. Coffee machine in the reception area.

"I'd have my secretary do it," he called back to me, "but she's at lunch."

Yeah, right. The last time this guy had a secretary, Rudolph Valentino was number one at the box office.

While Manny busied himself getting coffee, I walked around the room, looking at the framed 8x10 glossies of his clients on the walls. Clients like Elroy "Chuckles" Monahan; Clarence the Clown; and Jerry, the Animal Balloon King. Most of the pictures looked like they were taken decades ago. I suspected many of these guys had already gone to that great Comedy Club in the sky.

"You take cream or sugar?" Manny called out.

"Neither, thanks."

"Good, 'cause I don't have any. I have a packet of Coffee-Mate around here somewhere if you want it, though."

"No, black is fine."

"How about some Saltines to go with?"

He poked his head in the door and held up a crumpled packet of restaurant Saltines.

"No, thanks," I said, faking a smile. "I'm good."

He came back into the room with two styrofoam cups of what looked like motor oil.

"I'm afraid it's been sitting around for a few hours," he said, handing me my sludge.

A few hours? A few months was more like it.

"So," he asked, "you looking for representation?"

The springs on his swivel chair squeaked in protest as he sat back down.

"No, I'm a friend of Dorcas MacKenzie. Don't you remember? We met the other night at the Laff Palace."

"Oh, right," he said, recognition setting in. "I thought you were a comic when you walked in just now. The crazy hair and all."

"No, I'm not a comic," I said, through gritted teeth, wanting more than ever to wring Gustavo's neck.

"It's something to think about. You could be a female Carrot Top."

"Actually, I wanted to talk to you about Vic's murder."

"Oh?" He took a nervous gulp of his motor oil.

"Yes, I'm trying to help Dorcas clear her name. I think she's innocent."

"Really? So do I."

"You do?"

"Of course. I still can't believe they arrested her. She didn't kill Vic."

"Do you have any idea who did?"

"Absolutely."

I was glad somebody knew who the killer was.

"It was the mob."

"The mob? As in the mafia? That mob?"

"Yeah. Vic was a compulsive gambler. He was up to his eyeballs in debt. Vic owed big bucks to the mob, and my guess is that they were getting tired of waiting for their money."

"I don't know, Mr. Vernon. I seriously doubt the mob uses pantyhose to knock off their victims."

"I suppose you've got a point," he said, patting his comb-over to make sure it was still covering his bald spot. "So who do you think did it?"

You, possibly.

"I'm not sure, but I believe Dorcas was framed. I think somebody stole a pair of her hose and used them to strangle Vic."

I looked for a reaction, some sign of guilt, but Manny just sat there sipping his sludge.

"In fact," I said, "that's why I came to see you."

"Oh?" he gulped.

"Holly the barmaid swears she saw you getting something from Dorcas's tote bag the night of the murder."

"What?" He looked up from his sludge, alarmed. "That's not true."

"Holly says that while Dorcas was attacking Vic, she saw you bending over her tote bag."

"That's ridiculous," he snapped. "I was nowhere near her pantyhose. I was bending down over my own attaché case to get my ulcer pills. If you remember, I was pretty upset that night."

Indeed, I remembered how angry Manny had been to learn Vic was leaving him for Regan Dixon.

"After all I did for Vic, he tossed me aside like a used Kleenex."

He shook his head, disgusted.

"For five years I was on call for that kid, night and day. I cooked for him. I loaned him money. I changed the oil in his rattletrap car when he couldn't afford to take it to a service station. I even did his laundry. And that's the thanks I got. Just when he's about to make it, he dumps me.

"But I didn't kill him. In spite of everything, I loved Vic. He was like a son to me."

Suddenly the anger drained from his face, and tears welled in his eyes. Embarrassed, he swiped them away with the back of his hand.

"Besides," he said, pulling himself together, "I had a very good reason for wanting Vic to stay alive."

"Which was?"

"The only reason that counts in this town—money. Regan started negotiating Vic's network deal before his contract with me expired. Which means she would've had to split the commission with me."

"Really?"

"Of course. Ask any entertainment lawyer. Ask Regan, in fact. She'll tell you."

I intended to do just that.

"Well, if you'll excuse me," he said, "I've got some important work I need to take care of."

"Of course." I nodded as if I believed him. The only work this guy had was filling in *Mr Ed* for a four-letter word for "talking horse."

"Hey, you didn't finish your coffee," he said, eyeing my motor oil.

"I'm trying to cut back."

He swallowed the last of his, then took both our Styrofoam cups and tossed them in the trash. When I bent down to get my purse I saw exactly where they landed. On top of an eight-by-ten glossy of Vic, the glass frame smashed to smithereens. Vic's smarmy face smiled out at me from behind bits of broken glass and coffee splotches.

I quickly averted my glance, then got up and thanked Manny for his time.

As I headed down the creaky stairs and out past the Taboo Tattoo Parlor, I wondered if Manny might be the killer after all. He may have loved Vic, but if so, it was clearly a love-hate relationship.

And who knows? Maybe in the end, hate won out with a pair of pilfered pantyhose.

Chapter 15

Going from Manny's agency to Regan's was like driving from Calcutta to Calcutta Heights, or whatever the ritzy section of India is called.

The Premiere Artists agency was in a glass-and-steel fortress on Wilshire Boulevard, with travertine marble in the lobby, museum-quality art on the walls, and a parking garage that looked like a Mercedes showroom.

No framed photos of "Chuckles" Monahan here.

I found Regan's name on a directory and hopped on a brushed-steel elevator as big as my kitchen.

I shared the elevator with a couple of Armani-clad agents named Bree and Carlotta, who chattered about opening weekend grosses and their kabbalah instructors. Damn. Would I never remember to leave my elastic-waist jeans and T-shirts at home? Next to the Armani twins, I felt like a Kmart special at Tiffany's.

The elevator dinged at Regan's floor, which turned out to be Bree and Carlotta's floor, too.

A hatchet-faced brunette sat on guard behind a massive reception desk. Something told me I was never going to get past her without an appointment or an Uzi, so I walked as close as possible to Bree and Carlotta, hoping to pass myself off as a hotshot agent in elastic-waist jeans.

I was just about to cross the threshold to the inner sanctum when I heard a no-nonsense voice call out: "May I help you?"

Ms. Hatchet Face was glaring at me, her finger no doubt poised on the security alarm button.

"Oh, I'm with Bree," I said, with a careless wave. "I'm Helvetica, her kabbalah instructor."

She thought this over for a beat and bought it.

"Very well." She managed a brittle smile and waved me in.

I wandered along the hallway until I came to an office with Regan's name on the door. Inside there was a small secretarial anteroom, just like at Manny's place. Only this time there was an actual secretary at the desk. A younger clone of Bree and Carlotta, a sleek little number with perfectly coiffed hair and, as I was about to discover, all the charm of a pit bull.

I plastered on a smile, sucked in my gut, and headed over to her desk.

She looked up from the take-out lunch menu she was reading.

"Yes?" she asked, with more than a hint of impatience in her voice.

"I'm here to see Regan Dixon."

"Sorry, she doesn't read unsolicited scripts."

"I don't want to pitch her a script," I said, my smile growing stiffer.

"Well, she's not here. She's home today, in mourning. Personal tragedy."

"That's what I need to talk to her about. Vic Cleveland's murder."

"Are you with the police?"

I thought about flashing her my library card and trying to pass myself off as a cop, but I knew she'd never fall for it.

"No, but—"

"Then I can't give you her address. Office policy."

End of story. No further discussion. She went back to her take-out menu, studiously ignoring me.

So much for talking with Regan.

I was heading out the door when a cute young guy in a pinstripe shirt bustled past me to the gargoyle's desk.

"Hey, Meredith. You got a package for me?"

"Take these scripts to Regan," she snapped. "And don't dawdle."

"Yes, Sarge," he said, with a mock military salute.

I froze in my tracks. If this guy was going to Regan's, I was going to be right behind him, tailing him every inch of the way. I stepped out into the hallway and bent down, pretending to tie my shoelaces, which was a neat trick, considering I was wearing boots at the time. I waited till he passed me, then followed him out to the reception area.

As we were waiting for an elevator, we were joined by another pinstriped kid.

"Hey, Scott. Where you headed?"

"Gotta bring these scripts to Regan Dixon. She's home mourning for that creep boyfriend of hers. What a sleazoid."

"I know. Every time he came here he made me go to Starbucks and get him a cranberry muffin."

"I don't see what Regan ever saw in him," Scott said.

"Me, either," his buddy said.

Me, neither, I felt like chiming in.

The elevator door dinged open and we got on.

"Want to grab a quick lunch?" Scott's buddy asked.

"Sorry. Meredith is on the warpath. I can't believe I sweated my tail off for an M.B.A. to run errands for that bitch."

"Welcome to life in the mail room." His pal sighed.

We rode down to the lobby, where Scott's buddy got off, and Scott and I continued down to the parking levels. I kept my fingers crossed that we were on the same level. If not, I was sunk. But in a rare stroke of good luck, he got off at my floor.

I watched as he walked over to his BMW (apparently even the mail room guys at Premiere Artists drove luxury cars), and in another stroke of good luck, I saw that I was parked just two aisles away from him.

I leapt into Wheezy and followed him out the lot.

And that's where my good luck came screeching to a halt.

Scott sped off like a test driver on the autobahn. And there I was, stuck in Wheezy, the slowest car west of the Rockies. Scott had zoomed out of sight before I reached my first traffic light.

I pulled over and let out a stream of curses that steamed Wheezy's windows.

Then I had an idea. It was sneaky, but it just might work.

I got out my cell phone and called information for Amblin Entertainment, Steven Spielberg's production company. In case you're wondering how I know the name of Steven Spielberg's production company, remember: This is L.A. we're talking about. Busboys at Denny's know where Steven Spielberg works.

I phoned Amblin and asked to speak with Mr. Spielberg.

A soft-spoken woman came on the line.

"Mr. Spielberg's office, Carolyn speaking."

That's all the information I needed to know.

"So sorry. Wrong number."

Then I hung up and called Regan's office. The gargoyle answered.

"Regan Dixon's office, this is Meredith."

"Oh, hi, Meredith," I said. "It's Carolyn from Steven Spielberg's office."

"Oh?" Her voice rose an octave or two. "Really?"

"Yes, Steven read about Regan's terrible loss, and he'd like to send her some flowers."

"How lovely," she cooed.

"But I'm afraid we don't have her home address on our Rolodex."

"No problem. Here it is."

And just like that, she gave me Regan Dixon's Bel Air address.

What can I say? It pays to be sneaky.

Wheezy sputtered up the hilly streets of Bel Air, straining every inch of the way. It was like climbing Mount Everest on roller skates.

At last I pulled up in front of Regan's spiffy Tudor manse, just in time to see Scott roaring away in his BMW. I parked behind a beat-up yellow workman's van, grateful that Wheezy wasn't the only low-rent vehicle on the block. Although compared to Wheezy, the van looked like a Bentley.

As I headed up the path to Regan's house, I wondered if she'd turn me away. If she was anything like her secretary, I'd be gone in a heartbeat.

I rang the bell and hoped for the best.

Regan answered the door, and I gulped back my surprise. The last time I'd seen her, she was a tall, cool power broker. But today, without her designer suit and Jimmy Choos, she was about as powerful as a feather duster. She stood in the doorway, a surprisingly tiny figure, in a cashmere robe, clutching a glass of white wine to her chest, her eyes wide with grief.

First Allison. Now Regan. In death, as in life, Vic had left a trail of devastated women behind him.

I told Regan that I was investigating Vic's murder, carefully omitting the fact that I was working for Dorcas. And much to my relief, she asked me in.

I followed her into a cavernous living room professionally decorated in various shades of beige. She sunk into a pillowy armchair and gestured for me to take a seat on the sofa.

Somehow I thought she'd be surrounded by friends to comfort her and dry her tears. But it looked like her only friend was Mr. Chardonnay. Maybe it was true what they said about being lonely at the top.

"Want some wine?" she asked, picking up a bottle from where it sat on her coffee table.

"Not while I'm working, thanks."

"Oh, I understand, officer."

So that's why she let me in so easily. She thought I was a cop. No sense cluttering her brain with the facts.

She helped herself to another glass of wine, and before I knew it, she was pouring her heart out. I guess she really needed someone to talk to.

"I know Vic seemed a little rough on the outside, but underneath, he was a wonderful person."

Yeah, right. Like Idi Amin, with one-liners.

"If only I hadn't gone to New York that night. If only I'd stayed with Vic, he might not have been killed."

She looked up at me with wide green eyes. How pretty she was, even in her misery. Life sure isn't fair, is it? When I'm miserable, I get puffy eyes, a snotty nose, and Ding Dong crumbs on my bathrobe. But snot wouldn't dare show up in a nose as delicate as Regan's.

As she reached over to pour herself another glass of wine, her robe slid open, revealing an amazingly fat-free thigh, not an ounce of cellulite anywhere. For crying out loud, even her birthmarks looked good.

Of course, if I stopped eating all those damn Ding Dongs and worked out every once in a while, maybe my thighs would look good, too. Really, one of these days I had to start going to the gym. Just a few weeks on the treadmill, and I was sure I'd see a huge improvement. As soon as this case was over, I vowed, I'd sign up at the Y. Before long the pounds would simply melt away, and I'd have the slim cellulite-free thighs of my dreams. And no more Ding Dongs! Absolutely not. Except as a special treat. Or if they were on sale at the market. Or if I got really depressed. Or—

Suddenly I realized that Regan was looking at me questioningly. Oh, dear. She'd obviously asked me something, and I had no idea what it was.

"You wanted to talk to me?" she was saying. "About the case?"

"Oh, right. Yes, of course."

I asked her if she saw anyone go near Dorcas's tote bag, but like everyone else, all she saw was Dorcas trying to strangle Vic.

"Dorcas was crazy that night," she sighed. "If only Vic hadn't goaded her, he might be alive today."

"Ms. Dixon, I don't believe Dorcas killed Vic."

She looked up from her wine with interest.

"If she didn't, who did?"

"That's what I wanted to talk to you about. Are you sure you didn't see anybody go near that tote bag the night of the murder? Manny Vernon, for instance?"

She shrugged apologetically.

"I wish I could help, but I didn't even know Dorcas had a tote bag. And why are you asking about Manny? Do you think he's the killer?"

"It's possible. I was hoping you could verify something he said."

I told her what Manny had said about splitting Vic's commission.

"That's nonsense," she said, with an impatient wave of her hand. "Absolute nonsense. Vic's network deal wasn't finalized until after his contract with Manny expired. There's no way Premiere Artists was going to split that money with Manny.

"Personally," she sighed, "I feel sorry for Manny. That's the story of his life. He helps struggling comics get started and then when they make it big, they leave him. I'd like to give him a little something, but it's not up to me. You know what they call Premiere Artists on the street? The Barracuda Tank." She smiled wryly. "We didn't get that nickname by splitting multimillion-dollar commissions."

"Thank you, Ms. Dixon. You've been very helpful."

I left Regan in the hands of her good buddy Mr. Chardonnay and headed back out to Wheezy.

Very interesting, I thought as I chugged back into town. It looked like Manny Vernon was alive and well in The Viable Suspect Department.

Chapter 16

The last thing I wanted to do that afternoon was face Gustavo and squirm under the heat of his withering glare.

"He's awfully intimidating," I warned Lance when I met him outside the salon.

"Jaine," he said, checking his reflection in the salon window, "I'm a shoe salesman at Neiman Marcus. I've jammed size eight bunions into size six slingbacks and broken up fistfights at the Ferragamo 'fifty percent off sale.' You think I'm going to be intimidated by a hairdresser with attitude?"

He took my hand and led me inside.

"Don't worry. I'll handle everything."

He strode up to the reception desk, where the doll-like Deedee was making notes in her appointment book.

"May I help you?" she asked, looking up with a smile.

The minute she saw me and my orange frizz, her smile froze.

"I need to talk with Gustavo," Lance said, all business.

"I'm sorry," Deedee replied. "He's with a client right now."

"That's too damn bad, honey. I've still got to talk with him."

Wow. I never knew Lance could be so tough. Like Rambo, with highlights.

"I'm sorry, sir," Deedee said, her voice now a frightened squeak, "but that's impossible."

"Is it? Just watch me.

"Where's his station?" he asked, turning to me.

"Over there," I said, "behind the curtain."

And before Deedee could stop him, Lance was striding across the salon. By now all the stylists had stopped working. No scissors were snipping. No dryers were blowing. The only action I could see were a bunch of jaws dropping.

"Lance, do you really think this is a good idea?" I said, hurrying after him.

"Trust me, Jaine. I know what I'm doing."

He flung open the curtain to Gustavo's station, where Gustavo was putting the finishing touches on a customer's hairdo. Which, incidentally, looked spectacular. Why couldn't he have done a beautiful job like that for me?

If Gustavo had heard any of the ruckus, he wasn't letting on. He played it cool, working on his customer, his back to us.

"Hey, Gustavo," Lance snapped, "I need to talk with you."

Gustavo whirled around to face us, in tight black jeans and equally tight T-shirt, very little of his perfectly toned body left to the imagination.

Lance took one look at the guy and melted like a stick of butter in a microwave.

"Yes?" Gustavo prompted. "What did you want to say?"

"Oh," Lance gushed, "I just came to tell you what a great job you did on my friend Jaine's hair. Just super."

Now it was my jaw's turn to drop.

Gustavo looked Lance up and down and liked what he saw.

"Glad you approve," he said, with a sexy smile. "You should let me do you sometime."

"Why don't I set up an appointment right now?" Lance said, lobbing the sexy smile right back at him.

"Excellent idea," Gustavo volleyed.

Good heavens. Any minute now, they'd be lathering each other up in the shampoo station.

"I'd better go now," Lance said. "I didn't mean to interrupt."

"No trouble," Gustavo assured him. "No trouble at all."

Lance tore himself away from Gustavo and hurried back to Deedee to make an appointment.

"Nice seeing you, sweetheart," Gustavo said to me, snapping his curtain shut in my face.

My cheeks burning, I turned and saw Gustavo's clients buzzing excitedly about what had just taken place. They were lapping this up like puppies at feeding time.

"Give your tongues a rest, ladies. You'll wear out your facelifts."

And yes, I really did say that. I was that angry.

I stormed out of the salon and was stomping back to my car, practically breathing fire, when Lance caught up with me.

"Jaine, I'm so sorry. I guess I went a little crazy. Latin men have that effect on me."

"I hope you two will be very happy. Be sure to send me an invitation to the wedding."

"Let me make it up to you," he said, whipping out his cell phone. "I'm going to call a stylist friend of mine and set up an appointment for you. She's fabulous. I promise."

"Forget it, Lance. I've had it with stylists."

And I meant it. I just wanted to go home and spend the next year or so soaking in the tub.

But then Lance said two little words that made me change my mind:

"My treat."

"Oh, I can't let you do that."

"C'mon, it's the least I can do after bailing out on you like that."

Yeah, actually, it was.

"Please," he said. "I insist. It'll ease my guilty conscience."

"You sure this friend of yours knows what she's doing?"

"I swear on a stack of *Cosmo*s."

I thought of how nice it would be to be able to look at my hair in the mirror again without crying.

"All right," I said. "What's her address?"

I could always soak in the tub another day.

Everybody knows about miracle workers like Moses and Annie Sullivan and the guy who invented the Eskimo Pie. But here's a new entry for the Miracle Worker Hall of Fame: Lance's hairdresser friend, an adorable sprite named Susie Q. (Short for Quinn.)

Okay, so Susie didn't part the Red Sea or teach Helen Keller to talk, but she did—bless her adorable soul—turn me back into a human being.

When I first saw her spiky punk haircut, I had my doubts. It wasn't exactly the look I had in mind for myself. But two hours later I was a true believer. The ghastly Sunkist orange was gone from my hair; it was a rich glossy auburn, acres nicer than my real color. And the cut she gave me put that rat Gustavo to shame. She layered it for volume and blew it out into a glorious silken bob.

And so it was with a spring in my step and a dent in my checkbook (in the end, my conscience wouldn't allow me to let Lance pick up the tab) that I got in Wheezy and headed home on the freeway.

There I was, tooling along with a head of hair Meg Ryan would envy. What's more, traffic was light, a rare bonus in L.A. What a marvelous fairy-tale ending to the Gustavo horror story. Isn't life amazing? Just when you're ready to shave off your hair and join a convent, you discover someone named Susie Q and the world looks rosy again.

By now I'd gotten used to driving a stick shift. I'd forgotten how much fun it could be. If I had to buy a new car, maybe I'd buy myself a zippy sports model. It was high time I jazzed up my image; driving around town in my Corolla, I was about as alluring as Ethel Mertz on laundry day. Yes, it was definitely something to consider.

Filled with the confidence that only a good haircut can bring, I decided to test Wheezy's limits and put her in fourth gear. What the heck. I was on a roll. Feeling very Grand Prix-ish, I pulled the stick toward fourth.

But the stick didn't make it. No, to my horror, as I gave it a yank, the damn thing came off in my hand! Oh, Lord! There I was, on the freeway, without a stick, stuck in third gear!

I told myself not to panic. I'd just slow down and pull over to the shoulder. But did I listen to myself? Of course not. Before I knew what I was doing, I jammed on the brakes. Damn. Now the car was stalled.

Do you know what it means to be stalled on a Los Angeles freeway with cars barreling down on you at 65 miles an hour, praying they'll notice you in time to avoid a bloody crash? Yes, folks, it's one of those times when a six-pack of Valium would come in mighty handy.

I put on the hazard lights, and with trembling hands I tried to start up the engine again. But Wheezy wouldn't cooperate. Cars aren't meant to go directly from a standstill to third gear. That's why they've got first and second gears. A lesson I was about to learn, as Wheezy kept dying out on me.

By now sweat was cascading from my every pore. My palms were slick against the steering wheel, and Susie Q's glorious hairdo was matted to my scalp in damp clumps. Finally, after about the fifth try, the car started, with much bucking and snorting. It was barely creeping along, but at least it was moving.

That's when I looked in my rearview mirror and saw it. A giant SUV bearing down on me. I tried to wave it over to the next lane, but the driver was oblivious. He was going to rear-end me! Next to that monster, Wheezy and I didn't stand a chance. No doubt about it. I was going to wind up a tragic freeway fatality.

My knuckles white with terror, I clutched the steering wheel and gunned the accelerator for all it was worth. The SUV was so close I could see the driver in my rearview mirror. And yes, you guessed it, the idiot was talking on his cell phone! The dope had no idea that he was seconds away from a collision.

Just when I was convinced he was going to plow into my backseat, I finally gathered speed and managed to swerve onto the shoulder, escaping by mere inches what would have been a very messy demise.

It took a good ten minutes before my hands stopped shaking enough to call Triple A. And another twenty minutes before they showed up.

But I used the time productively, planning my 3.2 million–dollar lawsuit against Crazy Dave's Rent-A-Wreck.

Crazy Dave's eyes practically popped out of his head when I showed him the broken gearshift. He was so upset he almost stopped eating his meatball sub.

"It came off in your hand?" he said, his mouth full of half-chewed meatball.

"Yes," I sighed, "it came off in my hand."

"Not Crazy Dave's fault," he said, picking his teeth with his pinky.

"I'm not so sure a jury will agree with you on that one."

Reluctantly abandoning his sandwich, he grabbed a flashlight and headed over to where Wheezy was parked outside his office. He bent over the front seat, shining the flashlight into the gearbox, treating me to a bird's-eye view of his meatball-packed caboose. It made mine look positively waiflike.

"You have screw loose!"

"I know," I muttered. "For ever renting this heap from you in the first place."

"Somebody loosened gear stick," he said, emerging from the car.

"What are you talking about?"

"Somebody used ratchet to loosen the screws. I see scratch marks in casing. This was no accident, lady."

Suddenly I felt a wave of nausea. Could Crazy Dave be right? Maybe the stick didn't just happen to fall off. Maybe somebody tampered with it. After all, the door locks were broken. It would've been easy for someone to gain access and loosen a vital screw or two. No wonder the stick had been shifting so easily.

A chill ran down my sweat-soaked spine. If Crazy Dave was right, it looked like Vic's killer was out to get me, too.

I'd fully intended to rent my next car from Hertz or Avis, whatever the cost. But by now my anger at Crazy Dave had fizzled away. I was convinced that Wheezy had been tampered with. Crazy Dave's cars may have been wrecks, but I doubted they were death traps.

He sat me down in his office, while his butterball wife bustled about, getting me tea and baklava.

"Poor thing," she clucked. "You almost got killed out there!"

"Tell you what," Crazy Dave said, no doubt trying to stave off a lawsuit. "How about I give you an upgrade to a Mercedes? No extra charge."

He showed me an ancient Mercedes that was built when Hitler was in kindergarten.

"A beauty, no?"

No. But I took it anyway, and a half hour later I hauled myself home, exhausted.

"Oh, Prozac," I wailed as I shuffled in the front door. "You won't believe what happened. I was driving on the freeway and the stick shift came off in my hand and I almost got squashed like a bug by an SUV, and at first I thought it was an accident but it turns out it was sabotage, which means somebody out there is trying to kill me!"

She looked up from where she was sprawled out on the sofa and yawned.

So what's for dinner?

If that cat doesn't shape up soon, I'm getting a poodle.

I gave her a can of Hearty Beef Guts and was standing over the sink, eating peanut butter with my finger straight from the jar, when the phone rang.

I answered it warily, hoping it wasn't a telemarketer.

But it wasn't a telemarketer. It was Andrew.

"Hey, Jaine."

In spite of everything I'd just been through, I felt a surge of excitement at the sound of his voice.

"Oh, hi, Andrew," I said. Only it came out *O Hni Nand-rnew*, thanks to the peanut butter clinging to the roof of my mouth.

"You okay? You sound like you've got a cold."

Damn. Why couldn't I have been eating something sensible like low-fat yogurt?

"It must be the phone," I said, swallowing frantically. "Bad connection."

"I was wondering if you're free to get together tomorrow night."

He wanted to see me! That was the good news. The bad news came next.

"Sam's having a party at her place. You think you can make it?"

The last thing I wanted to do was party with Sam Weinstock, but the lure of Andrew was too great to resist.

"Sure," I said, trying to sound perky. "I'd love to."

"Sorry to call at the last minute, but I didn't know about the party myself till this afternoon. I'm hoping we can cut out early and grab some alone time."

If by "alone time" he meant some high-suction kisses in the back of his BMW, I was definitely available.

"That sounds great," I said.

Once again, Andrew was going to be working late, so we agreed to meet at the party. He gave me Sam's address, and I hung up in a happy glow.

I polished off my peanut butter dinner, scraping the bottom of the jar with my finger, then headed for the tub with a glass of chardonnay.

I eased my tired body into a tubful of steamy strawberry-scented bubbles and sipped at my wine. Before long I was lost in a daydream of me and Andrew at Sam's party, clinking martini glasses and feeding each other olives, then racing off for our "alone time" in the back of his BMW, Andrew looking hunkalicious in an unbuttoned button-down shirt, and me looking ten pounds slimmer in a sexy black cocktail dress, my hair a glossy cap of perfection.

By the time I got in my jammies and tumbled into bed, my body as limp as a lo mein noodle, I was twenty pounds thinner and moving to Stuttgart with an engagement ring on my finger.

Such is the power of a chardonnay bubble bath that I'd totally forgotten how—just a few hours earlier—I'd come *this-close* to being human roadkill.

Chapter 17

The next morning, I had no trouble remembering my brush with death. Ghastly images of my freeway ordeal came flooding back to me the minute I opened my eyes.

Like scenes from a horror movie, I saw the gearshift come off in my hand, the other cars swerving to avoid me, and the final terror of the moron in the SUV barreling down on me at 65-plus miles an hour.

I got up with a shudder and staggered to the kitchen to fix Prozac her breakfast, convinced that whoever sabotaged my car was responsible for Vic's death. The killer knew I was sniffing around, asking questions. Turning my car into a death trap was his or her quaint way of putting a stop to my investigation.

Who, I wondered, could have done it?

It had to be someone who knew about cars.

The first person who sprang to mind was Pete the bartender. His fingernails were certainly filthy enough to be an auto mechanic's. Was that one of his many job skills, along with bartending, bouncing, and selling X-rated videos? True, he seemed to have a most repulsive crush on me. But maybe that was just an act to throw me off his trail.

Then, just as I was nuking myself some coffee, it hit me. I remembered what Manny said about all he'd done for Vic. How he'd fed him meals and done his laundry and *changed*

*the oil in his car when he was too broke to bring it to a ser-
vice station!*

Could it be? Was Manny my saboteur? He obviously knew
his way around cars. Maybe, after I confronted him with
Holly's accusation, he felt threatened and decided to put a
halt to my investigation. And my life.

It was a nifty theory. But that's all it was. I didn't have a
shred of evidence to prove he was anywhere near my car—or
Vic's bungalow on the night of the murder, for that matter.

I opened my freezer and peered inside. Drat. I was all out
of Pop-Tarts.

I slammed the freezer door shut in frustration. I was no
closer to solving the case than I was the day I took it on. I
threw on some sweats and was just heading out the door to
revive my spirits with a visit to my pals at Krispy Kreme
when the phone rang.

It was Dorcas. In the background, I could hear the angry
sounds of women shouting. The words *bitch* and *whup your
sorry ass* featured prominently in their conversation.

Oh, Lord. How awful it must be for her in jail.

Any second now, she was going to ask me about the case.
What was I going to tell her? That I had scads of suspects,
but no proof whatsoever? That, far from nailing the killer, I
almost got killed myself?

But, much to my surprise, she didn't ask me for a progress
report.

"Jaine," she said, breathless with excitement, "come down
here right away. I've got something important to tell you!"

"What is it?"

"I can't tell you over the phone. Just get here as soon as
you can."

I hung up, suddenly hopeful. It sounded like Dorcas was
on to something. Maybe she remembered seeing something
at the scene of the crime, a vital clue that would lead me to
the killer.

I raced out the door and headed straight to the county jail.

(Okay, I didn't go straight to the jail. I stopped off at Krispy Kreme for a chocolate glazed donut. Okay, two chocolate glazed donuts. Are you happy now?)

"Well? What's your important news?"

I sat across from Dorcas talking to her on the germ-ridden prison phone.

She looked a lot healthier than the last time I saw her. Maybe prison food agreed with her. She smiled broadly.

"I've got the most fabulous idea for a new comedy act."

Huh? I tapped the phone, wondering if it was on the fritz. Did I hear that right? The woman had a murder charge hanging over her head, and she was talking about a new act?!

"I can use this whole jail experience as material. My Life in the Pen."

"But—"

"It'll be hilarious."

"But—"

"Look at Martha Stewart. She went to jail and got two TV shows."

"But—"

"Getting arrested might be the best thing that ever happened to me."

I just sat there, openmouthed, having run out of "buts."

"Dorcas, aren't you forgetting something?" I finally managed to say. "Before you can knock 'em dead with your act, you've got to get out of jail."

"Oh, that," she said, brushing aside my objection with a wave of her hand. "I know you're going to get me off the hook, Jaine. Ginnie Rae said so."

"Ginnie Rae?"

"My cell mate. She's a psychic. The tarot cards told her that her boyfriend was cheating on her, which is why she shot him in his privates. Anyhow, Ginnie Rae says I'm going to go free."

Great. If Ginnie Rae knew so much, let *her* find the killer.

"What's happening with your attorney?" I asked, trying to drag her back to reality. "Has he come up with anything?"

Dorcas snorted in derision.

"Are you kidding? The only way he's going to get me out of here is with a Colt .45 baked in a cake.

"What about you, Jaine?" she asked, finally taking an interest in her own welfare. "What've you discovered so far?"

That you're a stark raving nutcase!

I told her about Manny, my leading contender in the Suspects Sweepstakes, and how he'd been spotted near her tote bag.

"Manny? Gee, I never would've pictured him as a killer. But you're the professional, Jaine. I'm sure you know what you're doing."

That made one of us.

"The trouble is, Dorcas, you're the only one anybody saw at the scene of the crime. I need proof that somebody else was there. Think back to the night of the murder. Do you remember seeing anything unusual at Vic's bungalow? Anything at all?"

"No, the house was dark when I got there. I couldn't see a thing. I fumbled around for a light switch but couldn't find one. In fact, it was so dark, on my way into the living room, I tripped over Allison's violin case."

I sat up straighter.

"Allison's violin case?"

"Yeah. I almost busted my toe when I rammed into it."

"What was Allison's violin doing at the bungalow the night of the murder?"

"What do you mean?"

"She had it with her at the club, and afterward she claimed

she went straight to Hank's place and spent the night. So what was it doing at the scene of the crime?"

Dorcas's eyes grew wide.

"Omigosh. You don't think Allison's the killer, do you?"

"That's exactly what I intend to find out."

I rang the bell to Allison's storybook cottage and breathed in the heady aroma from her rosebushes.

"The door's open," Allison called out.

For a potential killer, she was awfully trusting.

I stepped inside and peeked in her living room, where I was surprised to see cardboard moving cartons scattered everywhere. The bookshelves were empty, the pictures down from the walls.

"We're in the kitchen!" Her voice came from the rear of the house. "C'mon back."

You'd think all those years living with a rat like Vic would have taught her to be a bit more suspicious. For all she knew, I was a door-to-door ax murderer.

I made my way down the hall and opened the swinging door into Allison's retro kitchen, complete with red vinyl banquette and a stove that was grilling flapjacks back when Ozzie was dating Harriet.

Allison, in jeans and a chambray work shirt, her Botticelli curls lassoed into a bandana, was busy wrapping dishes in newspaper and loading them into a carton. Hank was by her side, struggling to lift one of the cartons.

"Oh, hi, Jaine," Allison said, tucking a stray curl into her bandana.

"I see you're moving," I said, taking in the scene.

"Yes. Too many memories."

Totally understandable. I mean, it's hard to call a place Home Sweet Home when there's been a homicide on your living room rug.

Hank put down his carton with a grunt and began loading another.

"Hank got me an apartment in his building," she said, shooting him a grateful smile. "He's been so wonderful."

"Aw, it was nothing," he said, practically panting with devotion.

"It wasn't *nothing*, Hank," she said, touching him lightly on the arm. "It meant the world to me."

He was so flustered by her touch, he almost dropped a plate.

"The movers are coming at the end of the week," Allison said, going back to her dishes, unaware of the effect she had on him. "There's so much to do before then."

She loaded a final plate into her carton and sealed it with tape.

"So how are things going with your investigation?" she asked.

"Actually, that's why I'm here. There's something I need to talk to you about."

"Oh?"

She reached for a Raggedy Ann cookie jar on her kitchen counter and began wrapping it in newspaper.

"Dorcas says she saw your violin when she showed up here the night of the murder. I know you had it with you at the club, so I have to ask: If you went straight to Hank's and stayed there all night, what was your violin doing at the scene of the crime?"

"That's ridiculous," Hank snapped, his face flushed with anger. "Dorcas is lying to save her skin."

Allison sighed wearily and sank down onto the banquette.

"She's not lying, Hank. I was here that night. I slipped out while you were sleeping."

"You did?" He stood clutching a gravy boat, staring at her in disbelief.

"I wanted to talk to Vic. I was foolishly hoping I could

save our relationship. But he was dead when I got here, strangled with those awful pantyhose. I was so upset, I dropped
my violin in a panic and ran. But I didn't kill him."

She looked up at us with wide beseeching eyes.

"You do believe me, don't you?"

"Of course I do!" Hank said, hurrying to her side, love
oozing from his every pore.

And truth be told, so did I. I'd have to be made of stone
not to. I felt like a rat for even suspecting her. It was like ac-
cusing the Pope of shoplifting.

"I'm so sorry, Allison. I didn't mean to upset you."

"It's okay," she said. "I understand. It's part of your job."

"Well," I said, with a feeble wave, "I guess I'd better be
going."

I slunk out to the hallway and was heading for the front
door when suddenly I heard an earsplitting crash.

I raced back to the kitchen.

"Are you guys okay?"

"We're fine. Hank dropped my toolbox."

I looked down and saw a set of professional workmen's
tools scattered all over the linoleum.

I knelt down to give them a hand as they gathered them up.

"Are these yours?" I said, picking up a wrench that weighed
more than Prozac.

"Yes, Vic gave them to me on my birthday."

"What a birthday gift," Hank snorted. "Mr. Romantic."

"I didn't mind," Allison said. "I like working around the
house."

Oh, really? Suddenly I wondered if she liked working around
cars, too. Maybe Allison wasn't as innocent as she looked. I
was no automotive expert, but surely one of these tools was
capable of loosening the stick shift of a VW Beetle.

I headed back outside, utterly confused. On the one hand,
I simply couldn't picture Allison as a killer. On the other

hand, she had enough tools in that toolbox to dismantle Crazy Dave's entire fleet of Rent-A-Wrecks. She'd gone from suspect to saint to suspect again in less than twenty minutes.

I was just about to get in my rented Mercedes when I looked across the street and saw the little neighbor kid, the one who claimed to have seen Batman and his Batmobile the night of the murder. My expert eyewitness, still wearing his Batman cape, was running around his front yard screeching the Batman theme song at the top of his lungs.

I stood there for a while watching him run round and round in circles, going nowhere.

I knew the feeling only too well.

Chapter 18

At the rate I was going, Dorcas would be tried and convicted and working on her appeal before I discovered my first piece of evidence.

I really had to get a handle on the case. Which is why I decided to write out a list of my suspects. Putting everything in black and white often helps me clarify my thoughts. So I settled myself down on the sofa with a pad and pencil and a snoring cat. I got as far as—

My Suspects, by Jaine Austen

—when the phone rang.

It was Kandi, who wanted to meet me for lunch.

No way. Absolutely not. I couldn't spare the time—or the calories. Not after those donuts I'd had for breakfast and my date with Andrew just hours away. I had to work on my suspect list, and, if there was time, send out some resumes for an actual paying job.

No siree, I had scads of work to do; I wasn't going to loll around taking lunch breaks.

Yeah, right. A half hour later I was sitting across from Kandi at a trendy bistro down the street from her office eating something called a Nicoise Baguette. (Which is trendy L.A. bistro-speak for "tuna fish sandwich.")

"Any news about the Corolla?" she asked.

I shook my head. "Not a word."

"So you're still driving that awful Beetle?"

"Not anymore."

I told her about the Gear-Stick-in-My-Hands incident on the freeway.

"You poor thing! I assume you're going to sue the pants off Crazy Dave."

"Actually, Kandi, it's not his fault. Somebody tampered with the car."

"What do you mean? Who would want to tamper with your car?"

And before I could stop myself, I was telling her about the murder. I hadn't meant to. I knew she'd wind up lecturing me. And sure enough, as soon as she heard I was trying to track down a killer, she morphed into my mother right before my eyes. I swear, I could practically see an umbilical cord growing from her tummy.

"Not another murder investigation!" she moaned. "Are you nuts? One of these days you're going to get killed! And when you do, don't come crying to me."

"I just don't want to see an innocent woman in jail!"

"And I don't want to see my best friend in the morgue!" She took my hand and held it in hers. "Promise me you'll be careful."

"I promise."

"You know how much I worry about you," she clucked.

"Kandi, you're the best friend a girl could ever have and I love you dearly, but could you let go of my hand so I can finish my sandwich?"

With a sigh, she let go and I returned to my lunch.

"That reminds me," she said, reaching into her purse. "I almost forgot my Slo-Eater."

"You take that thing out, Kandi, and I swear, I'll punch its silly light out."

"All right, all right," she said, putting it away. "No need to get testy. I've mastered the art of slow eating anyway."

I'll say. She was still on Bite Two of her Chinese chicken salad.

"So what's up with the actress you hired to go to traffic school for you?" I asked, determined to change the subject.

She took the bait, eager to talk about her protégé.

"Miranda's all set to go. She's memorized the DMV handbook cover to cover. I can't get over how clever I was to hire somebody to be me. I'm actually thinking of having her call my parents for me once a week. Won't that be heavenly?"

Kandi was rambling on about the benefits of having a real-life stunt double when I glanced up and saw a familiar black ponytail at a nearby table.

It was Holly, aka Pebbles, the barmaid. She was sitting across from a muscle bound jock with delts as big as ham hocks. I assumed he was her new beau, the one she'd been getting ready to go out with the day I'd stopped by.

I watched as she slipped off her shoe and ran her foot up along his enormous calf. I wondered how high it would travel before lunch was over.

Then she slipped her shoe back on and got up from the table. She blew him a kiss, and he patted her on the fanny as she walked off to the ladies' room.

On an impulse, I decided to follow her.

"Be right back, Kandi. I'm going to the ladies' room."

"Remember to use a paper seat protector!"

What did I tell you? There was definitely an umbilical cord somewhere under her jeans.

I found Holly at the sink, putting on lipstick.

"Hi, Holly."

She whirled around and gave a little gasp.

The woman was clearly surprised to see me. Maybe because she assumed I was lying dead in the morgue with a stick shift clutched in my lifeless hand.

Then I glanced down at her lipstick case and it was my turn to be surprised. It was Dorcas's cloisonné lipstick case, the same one she'd taken out of her prop bag the night of the murder.

"Interesting lipstick case," I said. "It looks just like the one Dorcas used to own."

"Oh?" Feigning nonchalance, she peered into the mirror, fluffing her bangs.

"In fact, I think it *is* Dorcas's."

"Don't be silly. I bought it at Nordstrom."

"Nice try, Holly. But I don't believe you. Dorcas told me she had it custom-made by an artist friend of hers in Topanga Canyon."

I've got to give myself credit. It's a real talent, thinking up lies like that on the spur of the moment.

"Okay," she sighed. "So I lifted it from her purse. Like you've never stolen anything."

"As a matter of fact, I haven't."

"Well, goody for you. Alert the Nobel Prize people."

She dropped the lipstick case in her purse, along with the restaurant's liquid soap. She eyed their hand cream but decided against it.

It's a good thing the toilets were bolted down.

"Hold on a sec," I said, blocking her path as she headed for the door. "If you stole Dorcas's lipstick case, how do I know you didn't steal a pair of her pantyhose and use them to strangle Vic?"

And then, much to my amazement, that hard little face of hers crumpled, and she started to cry.

"Don't you get it?" she said, her voice practically a whisper. "I loved the guy. I could never hurt him."

She looked up at me, tears streaming down her face.

Were those tears real? I wondered. Was she really incapable of killing Vic? Or was she a kleptomaniacal killer who could summon tears on demand?

Once again, your intrepid investigator didn't have a clue.

* * *

Lucky for me, Kandi had only an hour for lunch; otherwise she'd still be eating her Chinese chicken salad. After Bite Nine she had it boxed to go, and we headed out to the parking lot.

"What a monstrosity," she said when she saw my Mercedes. "Are you sure it isn't a hearse? Sweetie, I wish you'd let me rent you a decent car."

"There's nothing wrong with this car," I protested.

She flicked a piece of loose paint from the fender and sighed. "Just be careful with your pantyhose murderer, okay?"

After promising her several times I'd be careful, I hugged her good-bye and watched as she hurried off to her Miata.

"Remember," she called back to me, "if you do something foolish and get yourself killed, I'll never speak to you again."

I climbed into the Hitlermobile and chugged out of the lot. Compared to Wheezy, the Mercedes was a virtual speed demon. Why, it could go from zero all the way to forty in fifteen minutes—with a good tailwind.

I was determined to go straight home and work on my Suspect List. If I hurried, I might even have time to send out some resumes.

As if. The next thing I knew I was in a Bloomie's dressing room trying on party dresses for my date with Andrew. I finally settled on a little black number with sequinned spaghetti straps, on sale for $120. True, it was $120 I didn't have, but how could I resist? It was short; it was sexy; and most important, it shaved inches off the dreaded hip-tush-thigh zone.

Flush with success, I paid for it with plastic and headed straight home to get some work done.

Okay, so I didn't head straight home. I stopped off at the MAC counter, where I picked up a new lipstick and mascara.

And Victoria's Secret, where I bought a black lace bra and matching panties. (I couldn't possibly wear that sexy black dress with a Jockey for Her sports bra, could I?)

When I finally got home I had just enough time to toss Prozac some Minced Mackerel Guts and grab a quick shower. After slathering my body with moisturizer, I got into my new black lace underlovelies and pranced around for a few shameful minutes, doing a very bad impression of a Las Vegas showgirl. Then I blew my hair dry and slipped on my new dress, along with my one and only pair of Manolos.

Finally, I slapped on some make-up and spritzed myself with some of my new perfume. (Okay, I stopped off and bought perfume, too. Sue me.)

I surveyed myself in the mirror. Good heavens. Who was that fetching creature in the mirror? Thanks to Suzy Q, my hair looked terrific. And my dress looked every bit as good at home as it did in Bloomie's dressing room.

If Andrew liked me with my Halloween hair, surely he'd like me even better now. I only hoped my new image would erase the memory of me showing up for lunch in an exterminator's van.

I headed out to the living room, where Prozac was snoozing on the sofa.

"Bye, Pro," I called out from a safe distance. I had no intention of getting cat hairs on my dress at the last minute.

Her eyes sprang open.

You're leaving me alone? You can't be serious! What if the apartment burns down? What if there's an earthquake? What if I get hungry and I eat up all my snacks?

She made her eyes go all wide and gooey and gave me one of her orphan-in-the-storm looks.

"Skip it, Pro. No guilt trip tonight. It won't work."

Okay, in that case, bring back leftovers.

Then she rolled over and went back to sleep.

In many ways, she was a lot like my ex-husband.

Chapter 19

As I drove up to Sam's house, a stately white mini-plantation dripping with magnolia blossoms, I felt like Scarlett O'Hara showing up for barbeque at Twelve Oaks.

I tossed my car keys to the valets at the foot of the driveway and headed inside, brimming with confidence. It's amazing what a little black dress and sexy lace underwear can do for a woman's self-image.

A uniformed maid greeted me at the door and led me to Sam's massive living room. I took one look around, and every ounce of confidence drained from my body.

Everywhere I looked I saw skinny women. It was my worst nightmare come true: a roomful of size twos. For a minute, I thought I spotted a size eight near the fireplace. Nope. She was just a pregnant two.

All at once I felt like a mutt at the Westminster Kennel Club.

I spotted Andrew in a corner talking to a regal blonde with an Audrey Hepburn waist and shoulder blades sharp enough to slice onions.

Every nerve in my body was screaming to get the heck out of there, to turn around and run. But before I could, Sam came floating up to me in creamy silk palazzo pants and matching cashmere sweater, the most elegant size two of them all.

"Hello, Jaine," she said, her eyes raking me over. "I see you've managed to fix the mess Gustavo made of your hair."

Huh? How on earth did Sam know about Gustavo and my Hairdo from Hell?

"You know Gustavo?" I asked.

"I'm a customer of his. A very good customer. Remember that letter you got offering you a free styling? It was a ruse, honey, to get you to the salon."

"I don't understand."

A nasty smile flickered at the corners of her mouth.

"Not very bright, are you, dear? I paid him to wreck your hair."

"You paid him?" I blinked in disbelief.

"An absolute fortune. Money down the drain, as it turns out," she said, eyeing my Susie Q cut. "I was hoping it would stay ugly until Andrew left town."

I stood there, stunned.

"You'd go that far to ruin my chances with Andrew?"

She shot me a look that could freeze ice cubes.

"I'd do that and a whole lot more."

Then she laughed.

"Not that I needed to bother. I can see that now. You're way out of your league, Jaine. Andy may think he's interested in you, but in the end, he'll come to his senses."

She plucked an hors d'oeuvre off a passing tray and took a miniscule bite.

"Better give him up now, before you get your heart broken. Oh, I almost forgot," she added with a feral grin. "Welcome to my party!"

Then she drifted off to join a clot of beautiful people with thin lips and tight jaws.

I felt physically ill, like I'd been slugged in the stomach. More than ever, I wanted to leave. But something in me wouldn't let me. That's just what Sam wanted me to do. I wouldn't give her the satisfaction. No, I'd stay and keep my date with Andrew.

So I sucked in my gut and marched myself over to where he was chatting it up with the blonde with the Ginzu shoulder blades. He looked cute as ever in his bizsuit, his hair still doing its irresistible curling-at-the-collar trick.

"Jaine!" he grinned. "I'm so happy you could make it. I'd like you to meet Gloria Otis."

"Hi," I said, forcing myself to smile.

"Hmm," she replied, irritated at the interruption.

Clearly Sam and I weren't the only ones who had eyes for Andrew.

"Can I get you a glass of wine?" Andrew asked.

Skip the glass, I felt like telling him. *I'll drink it straight from the bottle.*

"Yes, some white, please."

Andrew headed over to the bar, leaving me trapped with Ms. Uppity, who spent the next few minutes grilling me about my credentials, asking me where I summered (*the same place as I wintered—my backyard*), what club I belonged to (*the Macy's Panty Club—buy ten pair, get one pair free*), and what on earth a slob like me was doing at Sam's party.

Okay, she didn't really ask me the last question, but I knew that's what she was wondering.

"Well, if you'll excuse me," she said, "I see some people I'd much rather talk to than you."

Okay, she didn't say that either. She just murmured something about saying hello to Elspeth and Skippy and scooted away from me as fast as her skinny legs could carry her.

So there I stood, all alone in Major Wallflower Mode. If I closed my eyes, I was back in high school.

Andrew came back with my glass of wine.

I practically yanked it from his hands.

"Look what I nabbed," he said, holding out a plate full of hors d'oeuvres. "Munchies!"

I looked at the plate of piping hot yummies, and the will to live slowly seeped back into my body.

"C'mon," he said, taking me by the elbow and guiding me outside onto a beautiful stone patio.

It was a mild night, and the air was rich with the scent of night-blooming jasmine. We sat down at a wrought-iron table that cost more than my living room and dining room furniture combined.

"I hope you won't be cold out here," Andrew said.

"No, I'm fine," I said, taking a healthy slug of wine.

"Here, have a baby lamb chop. They're wonderful. I've already had three," he confessed, with a most appealing grin.

I had one, and it was indeed wonderful. So I had another.

"I'm sorry we had to come to the party," Andrew said, "but Sam insisted and I couldn't get out of it."

I just bet she did.

"Sam's friends are okay, I guess," he said, looking at the guests milling around inside. "But they're a bit too country clubbish for me."

"They are?"

"Yeah. They're a far cry from the folks I grew up with in Minnesota."

"You're from Minnesota?"

He nodded. "Duluth."

Well, knock me down with a baby lamb chop. He was an outsider, just like me.

And all along I thought he was born with a social register clutched in his tiny fist.

"Here. Try a crab puff," he said.

"Don't mind if I do."

I bit into a delectable concoction of creamy crab in a puff pastry shell. I thought I'd died and gone to Hors d'Oeuvre Heaven.

"You sure you're not cold out here?"

"No, I'm fine," I said, draining the last of the wine from

my glass. And for the first time since I walked in Sam's door, I did feel fine. More than fine. Yes, sitting there under the stars with Andrew and a plateful of crab puffs, I was feeling rather marvelous.

Just then I looked inside and saw Sam standing near the French doors glaring at us, her beautiful brow marred with a frown.

I smiled and waved gaily.

She quickly turned her attention to the group of people she was standing with. She pretended she hadn't seen us, but I knew better. She'd seen us, all right, and now she was doing a slow burn.

Eat your heart out, you vindictive bitch! I thought, savoring the moment.

Just as I was biting into another crab puff, I noticed one of the men she was talking to. A tall attractive man with graying temples. In a blue blazer and tan slacks. And tinted aviator glasses.

Wait a minute! I'd know that guy anywhere. I recognized the glasses. And the graying temples. And the blazer. It was the sleazy con man who pretended to be Stan McCormick—the creep who stole my Corolla!

Then, to my horror, I saw the woman next to him hand him her valet parking ticket! Holy Mackerel! Somehow he'd faked his way into the party and was pulling the same scam again! I couldn't let him get away with it.

I swallowed my crab puff and leapt to my feet.

"Jaine, where are you going?"

"I've got to stop that man!"

I charged through the French doors and saw my con man weaving his way across the room toward the foyer.

"Stop right now!" I shrieked. "I know what you're up to!"

But he kept on going, playing it cool, strolling out the living room, nonchalant as you please.

And suddenly all the rage I felt—at Sam, at Gustavo, at the

sicko who'd sabotaged my car—came to a head as I tore across the room.

"You miserable sonofabitch!" I shouted, tackling him from behind. "You're not going to get away with this!"

He was a big man, but fueled by anger and crab puffs, I sent him sprawling to the floor. Flush with victory, I straddled his chest, much like Dorcas had done with Vic at the Laff Palace.

Unlike Dorcas, though, I didn't go the strangling route. Instead I shouted:

"Somebody call the police!"

I looked around the room. But nobody reached for a phone. Everybody just stood there staring at me, slack jawed with disbelief.

I suddenly realized that, in straddling my con man, my dress had risen dangerously high on my thighs, treating the assembled guests to an up close and personal view of my new black lace panties. But I didn't care. I'd brought my car thief to justice!

Then Andrew stepped out from the crowd.

"Jaine, what are you doing?"

"This guy is a con man. He stole my car."

"Don't be absurd," Sam said, joining our little party. "He's not a car thief. He's Rupert Van Skoyk, the CEO of Union National Bank."

I took a good look at my captive, and my stomach sank. Seeing him up close, I realized Sam was right. He wasn't my con man, after all.

"Oh, dear. I'm so sorry," I started babbling. "I thought you were somebody else. You see, I went on this job interview and a man in a blue blazer and tan slacks just like yours with graying temples took my parking ticket and drove off with my Corolla and when I saw you take that lady's ticket, I just assumed you were my car thief."

"No," he said. "I was going out to the car to get my wife's sweater."

"I'm so sorry," I moaned. "Is there anything I can do to make it up to you?"

"For starters, you can get up off my chest."

Oh, cripes! I was still sitting on the poor guy's chest! I leapt to my feet, scarlet with shame.

"I'm so sorry!" I said, in what was rapidly becoming a mantra.

"It's all right, my dear," he said. And then he leaned in to whisper, "I quite enjoyed the view."

The CEO of Union National Bank had seen my black lace crotch. I wanted to die. I looked around and saw that nobody was looking at us anymore. They'd all gone back to their conversational klatches, talking among themselves. But I knew what the topic of conversation was: Me. Jaine Austen, Certified Crazy Lady. This was a story that would be circulating on the "A" list for months, if not years, to come.

"Thanks for the floor show, Jaine," Sam said. She and Andrew were the only ones still at my side. She could barely contain her glee at my humiliation.

Andrew, on the other hand, looked almost as mortified as I did. Poor guy. He'd never be able to live this down. It's a good thing he was going back to Stuttgart.

"I'm sorry I embarrassed you, Andrew."

He smiled weakly. "It was an honest mistake."

"No, it was a stupid mistake. A really stupid mistake. Wasn't it, Sam? It worked out so much better than a bad hairdo, huh?"

"What's she talking about?" Andrew asked.

"I have no idea," Sam replied, all wide-eyed innocence.

"Well, Sam," I sighed, "I guess you win. He's all yours."

And then I did what I should've done the minute I walked in the door. I turned around and walked out.

* * *

"Jaine, wait up!"

I was waiting for the valet to bring me my Mercedes when Andrew came running out of the house.

"Let's go someplace where we can be alone. We need to talk."

"No, Andrew. Sam was right about me. I'm all wrong for you. You belong with one of those size twos inside. You don't want someone in elastic-waist pants who writes toilet bowl ads for a living."

"But, Jaine," he said, as the Mercedes came rattling up the driveway, "I already told you. I'm not like these people. You and I have a lot in common."

"Really?" I said, getting in the car. "Would you tackle a bank CEO at a cocktail party? Would you drive around in a clunker from Crazy Dave's Rent-A-Wreck? Would you show up for lunch in an exterminator's van?"

He stood there, awkward and silent.

"I didn't think so."

Then I started the engine and drove off into the night.

YOU'VE GOT MAIL

To: Jausten
From: Shoptillyoudrop
Subject: Back in the Swing of Things

Hi, darling—

It looks like Daddy was right. The police haven't shown up, and I doubt they will. I guess they've got more important things to worry about than a ratty old shirt.

I know what Daddy did was wrong, but he's so much happier now that he thinks he's got his lucky shirt back. (For all I know, it *is* his shirt, but I sincerely doubt it.) Thank goodness he's stopped moping around. I thought for a while I was going to have to have him surgically removed from his La-Z-Boy.

The really wonderful news is that Daddy's membership in the clubhouse has been reinstated! He signed the contract at the board of directors' meeting, promising to behave himself, and miraculously managed not to offend anybody in the process. I was worried the board would find out about Daddy being the Shirt Thief, but everything worked out just fine. In fact, today is our first day back at the clubhouse.

This afternoon we're going to a lecture on Lowering Your Blood Pressure Through Positive Thinking (a skill I certainly could have used these past few days!), and afterward we're going square dancing. I'm going to wear my new Rhinestone Cowgirl pantsuit—a Shopping Channel "Bargain Buy"—only $45.99 plus shipping and handling. I can't wait!

Much love to you and precious Zoloft,
Mom

To: Jausten
From: Shoptillyoudrop
Subject: Kicked Out—Again!

You're not going to believe this, but Daddy's been kicked out of the clubhouse again!

Oh, honey, it was so awful.

We showed up for the lecture on Lowering Your Blood Pressure Through Positive Thinking, happy as clams to be back in the swing of things. There we were, sitting in the front row—me in my new Rhinestone Cowgirl pantsuit and Daddy in his "lucky" Hawaiian shirt—when Ms. Vickers, our new social director, introduced the guest lecturer, Dr. Herman Kotler.

Good heavens, I thought, where had I heard that name before? And then, when Dr. Kotler walked out onstage, I almost died! It was the same man Daddy attacked outside the Megaplex!

He took one look at Daddy and jumped down off the stage, shrieking "Shirt Thief!" at the top of his lungs. (I'm no expert, but he certainly didn't seem to be lowering his blood pressure through positive thinking!)

The next thing you know, Daddy and Dr. Kotler were wrestling each other over that darn shirt, each of them claiming the shirt was his. Thank goodness Ed Peters was able to pull the two of them apart.

Then Dr. Kotler took out his wallet and showed Daddy a photo with one of those camera date stamps, dated ten years ago, of Dr. Kotler wearing "Daddy's" shirt at a luau in Hawaii.

Even Daddy had to admit the picture proved Dr. Kotler had owned the shirt for years. He apologized to Dr. Kotler and had just given him his shirt back when Ms. Vickers started screaming. It seems that one of the shirt buttons had popped off in the scuffle and broke the cap on her front tooth.

She was so upset she quit her job right then and there.

"Mrs. Stuyvesant warned me about you, Mr. Austen," she said, "and she was right."

Needless to say, the board of directors kicked Daddy out of the clubhouse. This time, he lasted a whole twenty-three minutes.

Your thoroughly disgusted,
Mom

To: Jausten
From: DaddyO
Subject: Little Misunderstanding

Hi, sweetheart—

I suppose Mom has told you about the little misunderstanding at the clubhouse.

Your mother is so upset, I've booked us on a cruise to Bermuda to cheer her up.

I have to admit I've been acting sort of crazy lately, which is not at all like me. I finally realized that I don't need a shirt to bring me good luck. After all, the best thing that ever happened to me happened long before I ever got that shirt: marrying your mother.

I'd better go apologize to her.

Your loving,
Daddy

To: Jausten
From: Shoptillyoudrop
Subject: All's Well That Ends Well

Daddy just apologized. He was so sweet, I couldn't stay mad. And guess what? He's booked us on a cruise to Bermuda. Doesn't that sound lovely?

So I guess all's well that ends well. True, we'll have to wait another six months before they let Daddy back in the club-house. But on the plus side, I'll never have to look at that ghastly shirt again! And that alone is worth all the aggravation I've been through.

To: Jausten
From: DaddyO
Subject: Great news!

Great news, lambchop! The thrift shop called, and they found my lucky shirt! It turns out they never sold it, after all. They've been using it as a rag! I raced right over and got it. It's a little worse for wear, but who cares. I can't wait to wear it on the cruise!

Chapter 20

I woke up the next morning, Prozac curled under my chin. Who needed a man when I had a sweet loving kitty by my side?

Okay, so Prozac wasn't exactly sweet and loving. She was selfish and demanding, with the appetite of a sumo wrestler. But at least she never left the toilet seat up.

"Looks like it's just you and me, kiddo," I said, stroking her silky fur.

Then she got up and crawled onto my chest, and I got the scare of my life.

There on the pillowcase where she'd been sleeping was a dark pool of dried blood. My heart started racing. Had Prozac somehow cut herself? Omigod. What if the killer broke into my apartment in the middle of the night and, in another attempt to scare me off the case, attacked my darling kitty?

By now I was in an advanced state of panic. I was just about to scoop Prozac into my arms and race her to the vet when she began kneading my chest, the way she always does when she wants her breakfast. Funny, she didn't look hurt. I felt her body for blood. Nothing.

Then I sniffed the stain on the pillow and realized it wasn't blood, after all, but dried chocolate from the pint of Chunky Monkey I'd bought on my way home from Sam's party last night. I'd wolfed it down in bed, watching a *Six Pack Abs* infomercial on TV.

"Oh, Pro!" I said, wrapping her in my arms. "You're not hurt!"

No, but I'm hungry. So let's move it, okay?

"I'll get your breakfast right away, sweetheart."

The first thing I saw when I got out of bed (after an empty carton of Chunky Monkey) was my new black dress and lace undies lying where I'd left them in a heap on the floor.

I sighed. All that money for nothing. I'd never be able to wear that dress without remembering what had to be the most humiliating night of my life. I shoved it way in the back of my closet and tossed the underwear in my hamper, certain none of it would ever again see the light of day.

Then I shuffled off to the kitchen, where I threw my pillowcase in the washer and sloshed some Savory Sardine Slop in a bowl for Prozac.

Still hung over from my ice cream binge, I skipped breakfast (honest, I did!) and settled down at my computer to check my e-mails.

So Daddy was banned from the Tampa Vistas clubhouse. Again. I can't say I was surprised. Even worse, it looked like Mom was destined to live with Daddy's lucky Hawaiian shirt until death did them part. But on the plus side, at least Daddy realized how much Mom meant to him.

I sat there musing about the nature of true love and hideous fashion statements when it suddenly occurred to me that Daddy and I weren't all that different. He'd attacked a perfect stranger before a crowd of stunned moviegoers, and I'd attacked the CEO of Union National Bank before a crowd of stunned partygoers. I guess the nut didn't fall too far from the cuckoo tree.

A sobering thought—which was interrupted by the phone ringing. I was in no mood for conversation, so I let the machine get it.

It was Andrew.

For once the sound of his voice didn't thrill me. All it did was bring back unpleasant memories of me sitting on Rupert Van Skoyk's chest.

"Jaine, we need to talk. Please call me."

"Sorry, Andrew," I sighed. "No can do."

Andrew was an incredibly appealing guy, but we had nothing in common. I didn't care if he came from Duluth; he was on the "A" list now, and I was strictly a "C" list girl. Besides, what did it matter? He was headed back to Germany. Any way I looked at it, I'd wind up getting hurt.

There was no way I was going to return his call. I'd put him out of my mind and do what I should have done yesterday, instead of running around shopping for a dress I couldn't afford.

I'd get my act together and find Vic's killer.

So I settled down on the sofa with my pad and pencil and began writing.

My Suspects

By Jaine Austen

Allison. Sweet on the outside—but was she a killer underneath? Callously dumped by Vic; did she get revenge with a pair of Dorcas's pantyhose? And then, when I started asking questions, did she take out her trusty toolbox to sabotage Wheezy?

Manny. Another pushover on the outside. But had he been pushed once too often? After all those years nursing Vic through the rough times, did he go berserk when Vic tossed him aside for Regan Dixon? Holly claims he was sniffing around Dorcas's tote bag. And he knew his way around cars; was he the one who jimmied Wheezy's gear stick?

Hank. Head over heels in love with Allison. Openly admitted he hated Vic. Did he kill him to get rid of the competition? And yet the guy weighed about as much as my right thigh. Hard to believe he could come out the winner in a struggle with Vic.

Holly. No alibi for the night of the murder. Furious at Vic for double-crossing her. She stole Dorcas's lipstick from her tote bag; who's to say she didn't lift a pair of pantyhose, too? Did she live up to her Cute, but Psycho T-shirt and strangle her cheating lover?

Spiro Papadalos. Guilty of major fashion crimes. (Those gold chains! That horrible jumpsuit!) But murder? Not likely. No apparent motive. Vic generated business for him; why would he want to see him dead?

Pete the bartender. One of the cast of thousands who didn't like Vic. But why kill him? And why use Dorcas's pantyhose? Why implicate her when he was one of the few people in the club who seemed to like her? And most important, why were the world's biggest losers always attracted to me?

I looked over my list, discouraged. Nobody stood out as a prime suspect. I didn't care how much Allison and Manny knew about cars; I couldn't picture either of them strangling Vic with a pair of pantyhose.

As for my other suspects: Hank was too wimpy; Spiro actually respected Vic; and as much as I would've liked to put Pete behind bars and take him off the dating scene permanently, he simply didn't have a viable motive.

That left me with Holly as my leading contender. And yet, I wasn't convinced of her guilt. On the contrary, I had a sneaking suspicion she might be innocent. Those tears of hers in the bistro ladies' room seemed genuine to me.

So I was back where I started: nowhere. I'd cross-examined

everyone, but all I had to show for it were some guesses and vague ideas.

And then I realized there was one person I hadn't cross-examined, someone who might prove to be a very reliable eyewitness: Me.

Maybe I'd seen something at the Laff Palace that night, something I'd discounted, that would be the key to solving the murder. Could I possibly have noticed someone go over to Dorcas's tote bag and forgotten about it in the excitement of the ensuing drama?

I had to search my memory and go over the events of that night, beat by beat. For the next fifteen minutes, I racked my brain, trying to re-create the events of the evening, but the only image that kept flashing before my eyes was the sight of me sitting astride Rupert Van Skoyk's chest. That, and an Egg McMuffin dripping with butter. (Hey, what did you expect? I didn't have any breakfast.)

I got up from the sofa, disgusted. This would never do.

Maybe if I went back to the club and sat at the bar I'd spark a memory.

It was worth a shot.

Spiro's sports car was the only car in the lot when I drove up to the Laff Palace.

"Well, well. If it isn't Nancy Drew," he said when he came to the door, his gold chains glinting in the hazy sun. "How's it going?"

"Not so hot," I confessed.

"That's the breaks," he said. Mr. Sympathy.

"Do you mind if I come inside and sit at the bar for a while? I'm trying to spark some memories."

"Go ahead." He shrugged. "Spark away. Of course, you know there's a two-drink minimum."

Seeing my look of disbelief, he laughed and said, "Only kidding, Sherlock."

Just then a delivery truck drove onto the lot and headed around back.

"There's my meat guy," Spiro said, ushering me inside. "Gotta go open the back door for him. You know the way to the bar."

He flipped on the house lights and hurried off to take delivery of his Grade Z meats.

I made my way over to the bar and sat where I was sitting the night of the murder. At first all I could think about were the cockroaches that were no doubt scampering along the baseboards. But gradually, images from that fateful night started coming back to me.

I saw Dorcas bombing on stage, tossing bits of her pantyhose to the booing jocks in the audience. I saw those same jocks howling with laughter at Vic. I saw Vic taunting Dorcas and the other comics smirking at his nasty cracks. I saw Manny crumple in defeat when Vic dumped him, and Allison burst into tears. I saw Holly's face at the edge of the crowd, smiling when Vic told Allison he was leaving her. And Hank racing over to fight Vic—and then, shamefaced, chickening out. And then I saw Dorcas doing what Hank didn't have the nerve to do—lunging at Vic, her hands clamped around his neck.

That's the moment I needed to concentrate on. When all eyes were on Dorcas. Did I see anyone, anyone at all near her bag? No, all I could picture was the look of surprise on Vic's face, the rage burning in Dorcas's eyes—and that Egg McMuffin dripping with butter.

Drat. I really should have stopped off and had breakfast.

Obviously my stroll down memory lane wasn't working. I got up from the bar stool and walked over to Spiro's office to thank him and say good-bye. But he wasn't there. He was probably still in the kitchen with the delivery guy.

I figured I'd wait a few minutes, and if he didn't come

back, I'd let myself out. I could always call and thank him later.

As I sat down to wait, the phone rang. After a few rings, the machine got it.

"Spiro?" A raspy voice came through the speaker. "Are you there? It's me, Rocco. If you're there, pick up! It's urgent!"

Or, as Rocco put it, "oigent."

He sounded pretty desperate, so I hurried over to Spiro's desk and answered the phone.

"Spiro's away from his desk right now; can I take a message?"

"Yeah, sweetheart, you sure can."

It turned out Rocco was a race track buddy of Spiro's, calling with a bunch of hot tips. Not exactly my idea of urgent, but then, I'm not a guy named Rocco.

"You got a pencil and paper?" he asked.

I looked around for something to write with, but there was nothing on Spiro's desk except a half-eaten Danish, a photo of his mustachioed wife, and an issue of a publication called *Pussies Galore*. (Hint: It wasn't about cats.)

When I opened the desk drawer to look for a pencil, I saw something small and silver winking out at me. I froze in my tracks. It was Vic's phony "cigarette lighter," the recorder he used to steal the other comics' acts.

Thanks to my keen powers of perception, I knew it was Vic's right away. Mainly because it had his initials engraved on it.

"You got that pencil yet?" Rocco rasped.

"Sorry," I mumbled, "Spiro's joined Gamblers Anonymous."

Then I hung up and snatched the recorder from the drawer. I felt around and finally found a row of tiny control buttons on the bottom. I pressed the "Play" button, and the sounds of a woman in ecstasy (or faking it, anyway) came out through the speaker.

I'll spare you the tawdry details of what I heard; the only stuff suitable for publication in a family novel was "Oh, Spiro, baby!" "You're my big bad lover daddy!" and "I take MasterCard, Visa, and American Express."

I seriously doubted that the orgiastic gal on the tape was Spiro's wife. It was hard to believe his own wife was charging him for sex. Although I certainly wouldn't blame her if she did.

No, clearly Spiro was cheating on his wife. It looked like Vic had captured those illicit moments on his tape recorder and was blackmailing Spiro with his recorded lovefest.

Lord knows how long the blackmail had been going on. Maybe Spiro got tired of making payments and decided to put an end to it with a pair of pantyhose.

At last! A piece of evidence. An Exhibit "A"!

But I couldn't just stand there congratulating myself. Any minute now, Spiro would be finished with the meat man. I had to get out of there.

I tossed the recorder in my purse and made a dash for the door.

I peered into the hallway, relieved to see no sign of Spiro, then hurried to the exit, praying I didn't run into him. My prayers were answered. I slipped outside and was just about to head for my Mercedes when I noticed Spiro's sports car.

For the first time it hit me that it wasn't just any sports car, but a Lamborghini—long and low slung and exotic, like something from a futuristic comic strip.

And then I flashed on Allison's neighbor, the little kid in the Batman suit who swore he saw the Batmobile the night of the murder. He really *did* see a car outside Vic's bungalow that night. But the "Batmobile" he saw was Vic's Lamborghini!

Just then I felt a searing pain in my shoulder socket.

"You left without saying good-bye," Spiro hissed in my ear as he twisted my arm practically to the breaking point.

I began screaming for help, but my cries were drowned out by the belching of a passing bus.

He yanked me back in the club and slammed the door shut. I kept on screaming, hoping the meat man might hear me.

"You're wasting your breath," Spiro said. "The delivery guy already left."

He shoved me into his office and down onto a chair.

I eyed the door, wondering if I could make a break for it.

"Don't even think about it," he said, grabbing the baseball bat he kept behind his desk.

Then he held out his open palm.

"Okay, hand it over."

"Hand what over?" I said, doing a very bad job of trying to look innocent.

"The recorder. I know you have it."

"Really," I blinked, "I don't know what you're talking about."

"Listen, Sherlock. The next time you swipe something from someone's drawer, remember to shut the drawer. Don't leave it wide open."

Ouch. Game over.

Reluctantly I handed him the recorder.

"I guess you heard the tape," he said.

I nodded.

"Can you believe it?" Spiro scratched his hair transplants, incredulous. "After I gave Vic his start in the business, the ungrateful sonofabitch was blackmailing me! He threatened to play the tape for my wife unless I forked over ten grand. And I couldn't let that happen."

He picked up the photo of his wife with her stiff smile and faint mustache.

"She's not much to look at. But she's got an inner beauty.

"And," he added, with a nauseating wink, "a father worth

six billion dollars. You ever hear of Abe Bajanian, the Pita King?"

I shook my head.

"Sells pita bread to every grocery chain in the country. I wasn't about to lose any of that in a messy divorce. I had to do something."

"So you drove over to Vic's bungalow and strangled him," I said, wondering how the heck I was going to get out of there without getting bludgeoned to death with the baseball bat.

He barked out a bitter laugh.

"No, I didn't kill him. I thought about it, but in the end I didn't want to risk it. I stopped by the bungalow, but only to pay him off. Wrote out a check for ten grand on the spot. He gave me the tape and threw in the tape recorder. What a sport. I guess he figured he wouldn't need to steal jokes anymore, not with a staff of network writers on his payroll.

"I knew I hadn't heard the last of him. The guy was no dummy; surely he'd made copies of the tape. But what the heck." He barked out another laugh. "I can afford it. Thanks to the pita bread king."

A reasonable story, but I wasn't convinced. A guy like Spiro wouldn't want Vic hanging around dangling incriminating evidence over his head for years to come. No, a guy like Spiro would want Vic out of the way for good.

"It's the truth," he said, as if sensing my doubts. "When I left Vic he was alive and rotten as ever."

"Do you mind my asking where you were at the time of the murder?"

"Not at all. I was at Pete the bartender's, watching porno flicks."

At last. I'd met a husband worse than The Blob.

"If you don't believe me, ask Pete. He'll back me up."

I was sure he would. Spiro was Pete's boss. The guy who

signed his paycheck every week. A lowlife like Pete would be happy to lie for Spiro and give him an alibi.

Not that I didn't believe Spiro hung out at Pete's place to watch porn. The guy was probably a charter member of Dirtbags Anonymous. I just didn't think he was there the night of the murder.

But I couldn't let Spiro see how I felt if I expected to get out of there in one piece.

"Well, that all makes perfect sense." I tried my best to sound like I believed him. "So can I go now?"

"Not so fast," he said, blocking my exit with his baseball bat. "You're not going to do anything foolish like go to the cops with what I just told you, are you?"

"Of course not!" I lied, wondering how quickly I could get to the nearest police station.

"You'd better not. Because I'll deny everything. I plan to destroy the recorder the minute you leave.

"One word to anybody," he said, leaning in to me so close I could see flecks of Danish in his chest hair, "and you're history."

With that, he swung the bat with ferocious force—missing my skull by mere inches.

So much for going to the cops.

Chapter 21

I headed out to the Mercedes, my knees shaking like a pair of maracas.

No doubt about it. Spiro was my man. The guy had "killer" written all over him. He had motive and opportunity. Plus he was strong enough to fell an ox. Too bad he was about to destroy my one and only piece of evidence. I was certain Vic's recorder would be trashed within the hour.

How the heck was I going to nail the guy?

My only chance was Pete the bartender.

Spiro was probably calling him at that very moment and dictating his alibi. Somehow I had to wring the truth out of Pete and get him to admit that Spiro was nowhere near his place at the time of the murder.

I climbed in the Mercedes and began rooting around in my purse for Pete's business card. Finally I found it at the bottom of my purse, underneath some Life Savers. I fished it out gingerly. I only hoped it hadn't contaminated the Life Savers.

Then I got out my cell phone and punched in his number. He answered on the first ring.

"Hey, babe," he crooned, low and breathy, his idea of sexy—and my idea of an obscene phone caller. "I was just talking to Spiro. He said you might call."

"Is it okay if I stop by? I'd like to talk to you."

"Sure, babe—but I hope we do more than just talk."

In your dreams, buster.

"So," I chirped, ignoring his sledgehammer innuendo, "how do I get to your place?"

He gave me directions to his "pad" out in Laurel Canyon.

"See you soon," he said, his voice as slimy as axle grease. "I'll leave the lights low and my expectations high."

Ugh. Just listening to him made me want to wash my ear out with soap. Somehow I managed to say good-bye without gagging.

Before heading out to Laurel Canyon, I drove over to McDonald's for an Egg McMuffin. I simply couldn't face Pete on an empty stomach.

It was almost noon when I got there.

"Sorry," the lady behind the counter said, "we stopped serving Egg McMuffins an hour ago."

A weary middle-aged woman with tightly permed hair, she looked out of place among her teenage coworkers.

"Couldn't you whip one up?" I begged. "I've been lusting for one all morning."

"Yeah, well, I've been lusting for George Clooney all morning, honey. I guess it's not gonna happen for either of us."

It seemed like everywhere I went lately I was running into comedians.

I sighed and ordered a Quarter Pounder and fries—with extra onions on my burger, in case Pete got too chummy.

A half hour later, I was driving up the steep, torturously winding roads of Laurel Canyon, a rustic retreat popular with artists and performers and people who don't mind taking hairpin curves at fifty miles an hour.

Not that I was going fifty. The Hitlermobile was struggling to hit thirty, groaning every inch of the way, leaving a colorful trail of exhaust fumes in its wake. On level ground it had behaved relatively well, but now that it faced an uphill challenge, it was clearly showing its age. The last time the car had successfully navigated a steep incline was probably at Berchtesgaden.

I followed Pete's directions to the letter, and in no time I was lost. I must've run into at least five dead ends looking for his street. After cursing Pete out for giving me such crummy directions, I pulled over to the side of the road, hoping there was a street map in the glove compartment.

But when I tried to open the glove compartment door, the damn thing came off in my hand. I tossed it on the floor, hurling a few choice epithets at Crazy Dave and his wreckmobiles.

Luckily, though, I did find a map inside—along with a piece of petrified baklava.

I managed to locate Pete's street on the map, and five minutes later I was pulling up in front of a rundown cabin on a deserted cul de sac.

The cabin looked like something out of a Charles Manson photo album. Choked by overgrown shrubbery and infested with wood rot—I could practically hear the termites munching away at the foundation.

Worst of all, there wasn't another house in sight.

Suddenly I was nervous. Pete was a big guy. With dirty fingernails and a penchant for pornography. I didn't like the idea of being alone with him in this isolated cabin. Not one bit.

But I couldn't wimp out now. If things got dicey, I'd just have to fight him off with my trusty hair spray. Yes, I know most women use mace, but I've found Extra Hold Aqua Net works just as well.

I checked my purse, reassured to find my Aqua Net ready for action, then got out of the car and headed up the steps to the front door of the cabin.

I took a deep breath, hoping it reeked of onions, and knocked.

Pete came to the door in jeans and a stained undershirt. I was so glad he decided to dress for the occasion.

"C'mon in," he said, waving me inside. "I made you a martini." Then he added, with a most repulsive leer, "To get you in the mood."

If he wanted to get me in the mood to throw up, it was working.

I followed him into a living room decorated in what I can only describe as Biker Bar Grunge. Lots of black leather, accented by the occasional empty beer can under the furniture.

Dominating the room was a monster-screen TV, which took up nearly an entire wall. And gracing the screen was a nubile young blonde in a lab coat.

"Vintage porn," Pete said, pointing to the screen with pride. "A collector's item. You're gonna love it."

As I was soon to discover, this "collector's item" was a mind-defying opus about a nuclear physicist named Desiree and her rocket scientist boyfriend Randy. I didn't want to question its authenticity, but it was the first time I'd ever seen a nuclear physicist in platform wedgies and a rocket scientist with a nose ring.

"I've got one of the biggest collections of pornography in the country," Pete boasted.

Is that so? Your mother must be very proud.

I managed a weak, "How interesting."

"Let me show you something."

As long as it's not you, naked.

I tried not to flinch as he took my elbow. He led me out into a hallway lined with floor-to-ceiling shelves, all of them jammed with videos and DVDs.

"I've got over five hundred movies!"

And would you believe? Not one of them was *The Sound of Music.*

I glanced at the titles on the shelves: *Lawrence Does Arabia. Rosemary's Booby. When Harry Nailed Sally.* And others way too tacky to repeat to a reader of your delicate sensibilities.

"C'mon," he said, steering me back into the living room. "Let's get comfy."

He gestured to a worn black leather sofa patched in several places with duct tape.

I sat down, making a mental note to fumigate my outfit the minute I got home.

"Here's your martini," he said, handing me a drink big enough to get Seabiscuit snockered.

"I can't," I said coyly. "Not unless you have one, too."

I smiled what I hoped was an encouraging smile.

"Great minds think alike," he said, picking up a martini from where he'd left it on an end table. "Hope you don't mind. I started without you."

No, I didn't mind. Not at all. In fact, Pete had unwittingly come up with the answer to my problem; I'd get him drunk and loosen his tongue. And when his defenses were down, I'd get him to tell me the truth about Spiro.

"So what did you want to ask me?" he said, plopping down next to me on the sofa, his answers all rehearsed and ready to go.

But this was way too soon; he wasn't drunk yet.

"So you like erotic movies," I said, evading his question.

I looked up at the blonde on the screen, who had taken off her lab coat and was now splitting atoms in her thong underwear.

What was it about these porn actresses? Occasionally I'd come across them on the Whoopsie Doodle Channel in the middle of the night. They all had the same generic sex kitten face, the same dead look in their eyes. And this blonde was no exception; she looked like every other X-rated blonde I'd zapped past on my way to a *Lucy* rerun.

"Oh, sure," Pete said. "I love porn. How about you?"

"Actually, I haven't seen all that many of them."

"We've got to do something about that," he said, inching closer to me. "Now drink up."

"You, too," I said, wagging a playful finger at him.

I faked a sip of my martini and watched with satisfaction as he took a healthy slug of his.

"Like I said, this one is a real collector's item. Made about ten years ago. It's out of circulation now. Can't get it anywhere."

The blonde was now totally naked and going at it hot and heavy with Randy, the rocket scientist.

"Oh, Sugar Buns! Sugar Buns!" Randy was calling out in ecstasy.

"Sugar Buns?" I repeated.

"Yeah," Pete said, "that's the name of the movie."

Where had I heard that name before?

And then it hit me. That's what Vic had called Regan at the Laff Palace. I remembered how inappropriate it had seemed at the time, calling an ice princess like Regan *Sugar Buns*.

I took another look at the blonde up on the screen. Good heavens. No wonder she looked familiar. I *had* seen her before. Not on the Whoopsie Doodle channel. But in Bel Air. That young girl up on the screen, doing obscene things with a Bunsen burner, was Regan Dixon. Ten years younger, and a lot trashier. But it was Regan, all right.

I looked at her legs, wrapped around her costar's torso. They were the same spectacular legs I saw that day in Regan's house in Bel Air when her robe slipped open—right down to the birthmarks on her thighs! And now those same birthmarks were pulsating with fake passion on Pete's monster TV.

Regan had clearly done a makeover on herself over the years, smoothing out the rough edges and honing herself into a classic beauty. But I was certain that "Sugar Buns" and Regan Dixon were one and the same.

Suddenly a whole new scenario sprang up in my mind. All along I'd assumed that Regan—like Allison and Dorcas and Holly before her—had fallen under Vic's spell. But what if

Regan never loved him? What if he'd never won her over with his oily charm? Vic obviously had known about her porno past. What if he'd been blackmailing her into their professional and romantic relationships? What if he'd threatened to expose her unless she hooked up with him? And if Vic had been blackmailing her, Regan Dixon had a perfect motive for murder!

I'd come to Pete's cabin certain Spiro was the killer, and suddenly Regan had taken over as my Prime Suspect.

"Hey, babe." Pete's voice jolted me back to the cabin. "You in the mood yet?"

I looked over and saw, to my disgust, that Pete had taken off his jeans and was sitting beside me in a pair of Hot Lips boxer shorts.

Oh, puke. I had to get that tape, and get out of there— fast!

"Actually," I said, lowering my eyes, geisha style. "I'm sort of shy. I don't usually rush into things like this."

"Don't worry, doll," he leered. "You're gonna love it. I've never had any complaints before."

That's because inflatable dolls don't talk.

"You know what really gets me in the mood?" I said.

He lit up with interest.

"What?"

"This may sound strange, but do you have any tuna fish?"

"Yeah. You want me to rub some on you? Sounds kinky!"

"No, no. Could you make me a tuna sandwich?"

"You're kidding, right?" He scratched his underarms, puzzled.

"I know it sounds crazy, but it turns me on."

"You're nutty, you know that?" Then he winked. "Lucky for you, I like nutty. You sit right there and finish your martini. I'll go make you that sandwich."

The minute he was gone I dashed over to the VCR to take *Sugar Buns* out of the machine.

Just as the machine was spitting it out, I heard:

"Hey, babe, I'm all out of bread. All I got's hot dog buns."

I looked up and saw Pete standing in the doorway.

Damn. I was hoping that sandwich would keep him busy for at least five minutes.

"That's okay," I stammered. "A hot dog bun's fine."

"Hey"—he looked down at the tape in my hands—"what're you doing?"

His hooded eyes narrowed in a suspicious squint, and a frisson of fear shot down my spine.

"To be perfectly honest, Pete, *Sugar Buns* isn't doing it for me. I thought we could try *Sex Vixens from Outer Space.* That looked really hot."

I was *thisclose* to needing a barf bag, but I tried my best to sound seductive.

He fell for it.

"Anything that turns you on, babe. I'll go get it."

"No, I'll get it. You go get that sandwich."

The minute I heard him back in the kitchen, I grabbed Regan's *Sugar Buns*. Then I got my own buns in gear and bolted out the front door.

Chapter 22

I was halfway down Laurel Canyon when I realized Regan couldn't be the killer. She was on the red-eye to New York at the time of the murder.

Then again, maybe she *wasn't* on that plane. Just because Vic dropped her off at the airport didn't mean she actually got on board. Maybe she got a flight early the next morning—one that landed her in New York just in time for a late-afternoon network meeting.

These were the thoughts rattling around my brain as I lumbered home, exhaust clouds spewing behind me. That trek up Laurel Canyon had taken its toll on the Mercedes. It was belching and coughing as bad as Wheezy. If the cops didn't find my Corolla soon, I really had to start looking for a new car.

When I got back to the apartment I found two more messages on my machine from Andrew, asking me to call him. But I didn't. Because I knew if I did, I'd just weaken and go out with him again, and eventually wind up checking into Heartbreak Hotel.

Instead I put in a call to Allison.

"Hey, Jaine. How's the investigation going?"

"Actually, I think I'm onto something."

I told her about Regan, and her colorful past as a porn star.

"Regan Dixon?" she gasped. "I don't believe it."

"It's true. And I think Vic may have been blackmailing her."

"That's not so hard to believe," she said, with a sigh.

At last, the scales were falling from her eyes. And not a moment too soon.

"Look, Allison, do you happen to know if Vic was into pornography?"

"As a matter of fact, he was. Hank and I found a whole stash of the stuff when we were cleaning out his closet."

"You did? Do you remember seeing a tape called *Sugar Buns*?"

"No, but the tapes are out back in the trash. Want me to take a look?"

"That would be great."

She put me on hold and went off to rummage through the trash. A few minutes later, she came back on the line, breathless.

"I found it!"

Bingo! Clearly Vic had seen *Sugar Buns* and recognized Regan. And from there—for a scuzzball like Vic—it was just a hop, skip, and a jump away to blackmail.

I told Allison I'd keep her posted on future developments and was just about to hang up when I heard a piercing scream at the other end of the line.

"Allison, what's wrong?"

"Oh, it's just Hank."

"Stop making such a fuss, Hank," she called out. "It's only a water bug. I'll kill it as soon as I get off the phone."

"He's such a character," she said, with an affectionate laugh.

I smiled as I hung up. It was good to hear Allison laugh. I bet she hadn't done that in quite a while. I had a feeling she was falling for Hank. At least I hoped she was. So what if he wasn't Mr. Macho? He'd probably make her very happy. Heaven knows, she deserved it.

And Allison wasn't the only happy camper in town. At last,

this case was coming together. I was heading to the kitchen to celebrate with an Eskimo Pie when the phone rang.

It was Dorcas.

"Hello, Jaine," she said, in a flat, listless voice. Quite a change from the last time I'd spoken with her, when she'd been bubbling with enthusiasm, practically planning her HBO special.

"Dorcas, what's wrong?"

"Ginnie Rae read my cards again, and the news isn't good. A scary skeleton in a black cape kept popping up. Anyhow, I just wanted to let you know I'm accepting a plea bargain."

"What?"

"My lawyer says that with time off for good behavior, I'll be out in ten years."

"Dorcas, don't do it. Trust me on this. Everything's going to be okay."

"Really?" she said, hope creeping into her voice.

"Really. Just hang in there."

I hung up and called the Opie of Mayberry lookalike who was passing himself off as her attorney.

"You can't let Dorcas plead guilty," I wailed. "I've got evidence that proves she's innocent."

"Hang on just a minute," he said. "I'm on another call."

Then he put me on hold. At least he thought he did.

"Mom," I heard him say, "I have to hang up now. I've got another call. It's that annoying private eye."

"It's still me, Opie."

Okay, I didn't call him Opie. But I came awfully close.

He got rid of his mom and came back on the line with me.

"Sorry about that 'annoying private eye' thing."

"That's okay." Who cared what he called me, as long as I got Dorcas off the hook?

I told him my theory about how Regan was the killer and how she never got on the red-eye, but caught a later flight to New York.

"Forget it, Jaine. The cops finally returned my call. I know for a fact they checked out Regan's alibi. After all, she was Vic's fiancé. And the partner of a murder victim is the first person the cops suspect."

I guess they were a lot smarter than I was.

"They checked the airline manifest, and there's no doubt about it—Regan was on a plane to New York at the time Vic was killed. Three flight attendants will swear to it. Oh, wait. Hold on, it's my mom again."

But I didn't hold. I hung up in a disappointed daze.

So much for my brilliant theory.

Poor Dorcas. I'd gotten her hopes up only to be dashed.

It looked like Spiro was my number one suspect again. But by now my confidence was shattered. If I was so wrong about Regan, who's to say I wasn't wrong about Spiro, too?

In fact, the more I thought about it, the less convinced I was of his guilt. Maybe he'd been telling me the truth. Maybe all he'd done to Vic the night of the murder was write him a check for ten grand. Besides, if he were the murderer, he probably never would have let me leave the Laff Palace alive.

I headed off to the kitchen to drown my frustrations in that Eskimo Pie. But when I looked in my freezer, all I found was an ice pack and a bagel with freezer burn.

Sucking on the bagel, I called Domino's and ordered a medium pepperoni pizza, with extra anchovies for Prozac.

While I waited for the pizza delivery guy to show up, I hopped in the shower. I wanted to scrub away every lingering molecule from Pete's cabin. But no matter how much I scrubbed, I couldn't erase the image of Pete in his Hot Lips boxer shorts.

And then suddenly I remembered the *Sugar Buns* tape. I'd stolen Pete's prized "collector's item." Sooner or later he'd discover it was missing. No way was I going to return it to him in person. I'd just drop it in the mail with a phony excuse about how it must've fallen into my bag by accident.

Prozac and I had our pizza in bed, watching *North by Northwest* on TV. Well, Prozac was watching (she loves Cary Grant). But I couldn't stop thinking about Regan. My gut kept telling me that she was the killer, although the facts were telling me she couldn't possibly be.

As much as I tried, I couldn't concentrate on the movie. Just when Cary and Eva Marie Saint were hanging by their fingernails from Mount Rushmore, I got up from bed and started getting dressed.

"I'll be back soon, Pro. I'm going out for a walk."

Oh, please. We both know you're going for ice cream.

"It shows how much you know, smarty. I am not going for ice cream."

And I didn't.

I went for frozen yogurt.

I was sitting at my local Penguins, slurping a chocolate-and-vanilla-swirl cone and wondering how I was going to tell Dorcas she'd been a fool to have faith in me, when my cell phone rang.

It was Kandi.

"Oh, Jaine. I'm so mad I could spit. That silly actress I hired to play me flunked traffic school."

"I don't get it. I thought you said she was so smart."

"She got a call to go on an audition in the middle of the class. And she went! She never even took the final test. So they flunked me!"

"Well, I hope you learned your lesson."

"I certainly have. I will never hire an out-of-work actress to pretend to be me again."

"Good."

"They're so unreliable. Next time I'll try an out-of-work writer."

"Kandi, you're missing the point. You can't go around hiring someone to do your dirty work for you."

And that's when the lightbulb went off over my head.

"Omigosh!" I shrieked. I was so excited I almost dropped my cone.

"What is it?"

"I know how Regan killed Vic!"

"Who's Regan?"

"I'll call you back later," I said, snapping the phone shut.

Yes, I finally figured out how Regan got rid of Vic. It was all so simple. Like Kandi, she hired someone to do her dirty work for her. Didn't Manny say he thought the murder was the work of a hit man? Well, he was right. Only it wasn't the mob who paid for the kill. It was Regan. She hired somebody to bump off her blackmailer. And carefully planned the murder for when she'd be on a red-eye to New York, giving herself an airtight alibi.

Then suddenly my elation turned to terror.

What if that hit man was Pete? Right from the start, I thought he looked like an extra from *The Sopranos*. I shuddered to think that I'd been alone with him in that deserted cabin of his. Maybe he had orders to kill me, too. Maybe I was never supposed to have left his cabin alive.

By now I was so scared I couldn't even finish my cone. Okay, I finished it, but I hardly tasted a thing.

I raced out of Penguins into the parking lot and checked the backseat of the Mercedes, terrified I'd find Pete with a garrote at the ready. But the car was free of hit men, so I got in and drove back home.

I had to get that tape from my apartment and bring it to the cops.

As the car trudged along, spewing smoke, I kept checking the rearview mirror to see if anyone was following me. As far as I could tell, nobody was.

At last I pulled up in front of my duplex. I was just about to get out of the car when I saw someone getting out of a van across the street.

Oh, Lord. What if it was Pete, come to finish what he'd started that afternoon?

But no, it was a much smaller guy.

With a sigh of relief, I got out of the Mercedes. Just as I did, the guy at the van turned to face me, and I saw that it was Hank.

What on earth was he doing here?

I took another look at his van and had the strange feeling I'd seen it somewhere before. And then I recognized it. It was the same beat-up yellow van I saw parked outside Regan's house the day I went to visit her. I remembered how grateful I'd been to see I wasn't the only low-rent driver on the block.

An uncomfortable knot began to form in my stomach.

Did Hank know Regan? He couldn't possibly be her hit man, could he? Wimpy little Hank?

But now, as he began walking toward me, he didn't look so wimpy anymore. In fact, in the glow of the street lamp, he looked sort of scary.

I told myself I was being ridiculous, that my imagination was in overdrive. It was just Hank. Sweet, harmless Hank. Allison probably sent him over with Vic's copy of *Sugar Buns*.

"Hey, Hank." I forced myself to smile.

"Hello, Jaine."

He had the same look in his eyes that Prozac gets right before she pounces on her rubber mouse.

I knew then that I wasn't imagining things. Something told me to run for my life. Which is exactly what I did. But Hank was faster than me. A lot faster. I didn't get very far when he grabbed me from behind.

"Get back in the car, Jaine. We're going for a ride."

I figured I'd better do what he said. Especially when he rammed the cold hard butt of a gun in my back.

Chapter 23

Hank grabbed me roughly by the shoulders and shoved me over to the Mercedes.

It was amazing how strong he was. What happened to the endearing wimp who was afraid of water bugs?

He pushed me in through the passenger door to the driver's side, then slid in next to me on the Mercedes' old-fashioned bench seat—all the while jabbing his gun most disconcertingly in my gut.

"Start the car," he ordered.

I reached in my purse for my car keys and felt my can of Aqua Net. For an instant I was tempted to blast him with it, but I couldn't risk it. Not with his gun just inches away from several vital internal organs.

So I obediently took out my car keys and started the car.

"Where are we going?" I asked, as the car sputtered into action.

"To the beach. Take Olympic Boulevard to the ocean."

My knuckles white on the steering wheel, I started driving. I didn't know exactly what was in store for me that evening, but I had a feeling it was going to end with my obituary. Hank wasn't forcing me out to the beach at gunpoint to take in the scenery.

I prayed that traffic would slow us down. But traffic was

lighter than I'd seen it in years. The cars were zipping along with nary a snarl.

Needless to say, the Mercedes wasn't doing much zipping.

"Where'd you get this piece of junk?" Hank sneered. "Mercedes of Baghdad?"

"It's a rental."

"What a clunker. Too bad you won't be around to demand a refund."

My stomach curdled. It looked like I was right about that obituary.

"So you figured everything out," he said, his gun still firmly lodged in my side. "Allison told me about your phone call. You know, you're not nearly as clueless as you seem."

I would've been insulted at that crack if I hadn't been so busy being terrified.

"Vic blackmailed Regan into being his agent. And as if that weren't bad enough, the bastard expected her to marry him, too. So I agreed to knock him off for her."

"But why?" That was the one thing I didn't understand. "To get him out of the way, so you'd have a shot at Allison?"

"Allison?" He sounded puzzled. "I didn't do it for Allison. Sure, I'd like to get her in the sack some day, but I wouldn't risk my neck for her."

"Then why did you do it?"

"For a movie deal, of course."

"A movie deal?"

I blinked in disbelief.

"I sent Regan my script, and she liked it. She promised she'd sell it to a major studio, for at least six figures. But first, I had to do her a little favor and bump off Vic."

He said this as casually as if Regan had sent him out for Chinese chicken salad.

"Let me get this straight. You were willing to kill for a movie deal?"

"Oh, grow up, Jaine," he said. "This is Hollywood. It wouldn't be the first time."

And you know something? He was probably right.

"Originally I was going to kill him with my gun, but when Dorcas made that big scene at the club, I figured why not grab a pair of her pantyhose and make her the prime suspect? Nobody even noticed when I lifted a pair from her prop bag; they were all too busy watching her trying to strangle Vic.

"Afterward, I played the part of the lovestruck platonic friend and invited Allison to stay at my place. A brilliant idea, if I do say so myself. She was the perfect alibi. I waited till she fell asleep, then drove over to the bungalow.

"I told Vic I was there to get some of Allison's stuff. He didn't suspect a thing. He let me in and went back to packing his suitcase. I waited till his back was turned, then whipped out Dorcas's pantyhose and strangled him. Sure, he put up a struggle, but in the end, I won."

I turned and saw a smug smile on his face.

"And the good news is, he suffered. If anyone deserved to, he did."

My mind was reeling. Did Hank honestly think he was the good guy in this scenario?

"I got back home and tumbled into bed, never dreaming that Allison would be going out to the bungalow, too. That wasn't supposed to happen. I gave her a sleeping pill to put her out for the night, but she never took it. It turns out she doesn't approve of Western medicines."

By now we were out on the coast highway heading north toward Malibu, and Hank began bragging about how he was going to star in his own movie.

"I'm one hell of an actor," he said, scratching his chin with the butt of his gun. "I had everybody convinced I was the original 99-pound weakling. You dopes all thought I was scared of my own shadow."

And I, of course, had been the biggest dope of all.

"I could've beaten Vic to a pulp that night at the Laff Palace, but I had to play the part of the coward. And it worked. Nobody thought I had the nerve to commit murder. And certainly nobody thought I was strong enough to overpower Vic."

I remembered the exercise machine in his apartment, the one he claimed he never used.

"You don't really use that Bowflex of yours as a coat rack, do you?"

"Are you kidding? I work out seven days a week. I've got muscles as hard as granite.

"Feel this," he said, shoving his arm in front of my face.

It made me sick to touch him, but I felt his arm, and it was indeed solid with muscles.

He admired his own arm for a bit and then continued with his story. He was loving every minute of this.

"I wasn't the only one acting. Regan was playing her part, too—pretending to be crazy about Vic, and then faking a broken heart when he died. Remember that day you stopped by to see her? Regan wasn't mourning. The two of us were celebrating; that's why the bottle of wine was out. When we heard you coming up the walk, I ran and hid in her bedroom."

He giggled at the memory, a high-pitched, strangely girlish laugh that, for some reason scared me almost as much as his gun poking in my side.

"Everything was going along so beautifully until you started nosing around. At first we just meant to scare you—"

"By loosening the gear stick on my car."

"Exactly."

"But then you figured out the truth. So now Regan wants me to get rid of you."

"What about Allison?" I asked. Thanks to me, she knew the truth, too.

"I'll probably have to kill her," he said, with a sigh. "Which is a pity, because I like her a lot."

My stomach lurched. Poor Allison. If only I hadn't made that phone call.

"We're almost there," he said. "Just a bit more to go."

We were out in Malibu now, and the traffic was still unusually light.

When we pulled up at a stoplight, I looked over at the family in the car next to us: a mother and father up front and two towheaded kids in the backseat. How I envied them their freedom, their long lives ahead of them. I wondered where they were going. To the movies? To get ice cream? Or were they simply on their way home to nice comfy beds?

If only I hadn't taken up this ridiculous private detective hobby. If only I'd listened to my mother and gotten married again, I could be living somewhere in the valley watching Must See TV, nagging my kids to do their homework, instead of driving off to what was sure to be a most unpleasant death.

Just then the woman in the next car rolled down her window and gestured for me to roll down mine. Then she held up a map.

Obviously they were lost and needed directions.

"Ignore them," Hank said, ramming the gun in my side. "Or I'll blow your guts out."

My first instinct was to obey him, of course. But then I wondered: Would he really blow me away in front of a car full of witnesses? Would he be crazy enough to take that chance? And even if he did, what did it matter? He was going to kill me in a few minutes, anyway.

So then I did the bravest thing I ever did in my life:

I rolled down the window.

"Help!"

I meant to shout but my voice came out in a terrified squeak.

"Call 9-1-1! This man is going to kill me!"

I cringed, waiting for an explosion from Hank's gun. But nothing happened. My gamble had paid off.

Far from being alarmed, though, the woman smiled.

What the heck was she smiling for? Did she not understand the words *this man is going to kill me?*

Apparently not.

"Sprechen zie Deutsch?" she asked.

Oh, cripes. They were German tourists.

"Don't you speak English?" I wailed.

"English? Nein." She shrugged with that maddening smile on her face.

Hank, turning in another bravura performance, ruffled my hair affectionately and laughed, like I'd been kidding around. Then, as soon as the light turned green, he kicked my foot off the brake pedal and rammed down on the accelerator.

"You crazy bitch," he muttered as we sped off, burning rubber.

Taking no chances, he spent the rest of the short ride with his foot on the gas pedal and his non-gun-toting hand on the steering wheel.

Minutes later, he steered the Mercedes off onto a deserted cliff.

I looked out at the ocean, black and forbidding under a starless sky, and heard the surf pounding on the rocks below.

"Here we are, Jaine," Hank said. "The end of the line."

He took the keys out of the ignition and got out of the Mercedes.

"Just a little precaution," he said, jiggling the keys, "so you won't try anything funny, like running me over."

Then he walked around to the driver's side and put his gun up against my left temple.

"Okay, Jaine. I've written a little scene that you're going to star in. In case you haven't already guessed, it's a tragedy. You're going to lose control of your car and crash through the guardrail down into the ocean. Better get it right the first time, because there are no retakes."

"Don't do this, Hank," I begged. "Don't you realize what's happening? You're taking all the risks, and Regan's getting away with murder. What if she doesn't get you a movie deal? You're screwed. You can't go to the cops, because you're the one who did the dirty work."

"Maybe I can't go to the cops," he smirked, "but I can tell the world about *Sugar Buns*. I've got leverage."

"Exactly. What if Regan doesn't like you having leverage? She hired you to get rid of Vic. What if she hires someone else to get rid of you?"

"Oh, come on. She'd never betray me like that."

"For crying out loud, Hank, she's an agent. They eat betrayal for breakfast."

For a moment I saw a flicker of doubt cross his face. But then it was gone, and his jaw tightened with determination.

"Forget it, Jaine. It's not going to work."

He held out the car keys.

"Either you start the car and drive over the cliff, or you get your head blown off. And this time I'll really do it."

I could tell by the look in his eyes that he meant it. This time, there were no German tourists on hand to witness the event.

"So what's it going to be?"

A cold watery death sounded dreadful, but having my brains blown out wasn't exactly a ride in the wine country, either.

With trembling hands, I took the keys.

My mind raced frantically. There had to be some way out of this horrible mess. And then I looked down and saw it: the glove compartment door. It was still on the floor where I'd tossed it the other day.

That was it. My way out.

Pretending to fumble, I dropped the car keys.

"Sorry," I said. "I'm so nervous."

"Just pick them up," Hank sighed impatiently.

I bent down as if to get them.

"I can't find them."

"Oh, for Pete's sake," Hank said and put his head in the car to get a better look.

Which was exactly what I hoped he'd do. Wasting no time, I grabbed the glove compartment door and whacked him in the head as hard as I could.

He reeled back from the car, stunned, the gun falling from his hand.

I sprinted out of the car and dove for where it had clattered on the pavement. I'd just grabbed it when Hank lunged at me from behind. I fought him off with every ounce of strength in my body. But I was no match for the ferocity of a screenwriter desperate for a movie deal.

In no time, he'd wrested the gun from my grasp and was shoving it back in its old familiar resting place: my gut.

"I've had enough of your games," he said, his eyes blazing with fury. "The party's over, Jaine."

Then he aimed the gun at my forehead.

Oh, Lord. This was it. This really was the end of the road.

Suddenly I was blinded by a fierce white light.

Had Hank pulled the trigger? Was I dead? Was this the after-death white light I'd read so much about?

And then I heard someone shout: "Freeze!"

I looked up and, to my immense relief, I realized that I was still alive and that the white light blinding me was coming from the headlights of a squad car.

Two cops had their guns drawn, aiming at Hank.

That blessed German woman must've understood me, after all, and called the cops.

"Drop the gun!" one of the cops shouted.

Meek as a puppy, Hank dropped the gun, and the next thing I knew he was up against the squad car spread-eagled and handcuffed—and ratting on Regan before the cuffs were even locked.

Ten minutes later, the place was swarming with squad cars, and a sweet officer with a blond ponytail was pouring me a cup of coffee from her thermos.

The cop who'd put the cuffs on Hank came over to ask me how I was doing. I started babbling an endless stream of thank yous.

"Thank heavens you came when you did," I said, shuddering at the thought of what would have happened had he shown up thirty seconds later.

"You're lucky that lady called to tell us about you."

"Oh, yes," I said. "The German tourist."

"German tourist? What German tourist?"

"Didn't you get a 9-1-1 call from a German tourist?"

"No, we got a call from an angry environmentalist, reporting an old Mercedes spewing carcinogens on the coast highway."

"And that's why you tracked me down?"

He nodded.

God bless Crazy Dave and his wreckmobiles!

"Is there anything else we can get you, ma'am?" the cop asked.

"No, I'm just happy to be alive on the planet to see the dawn of a new day."

Okay, so what I really said was:

"Got any chocolate?"

Chapter 24

It was after midnight when I finally staggered home. Prozac looked up from where she was curled on my pillow and yawned.

Did you bring me ice cream?

"Are you kidding? You're lucky I'm alive. I almost got my head blown off by a sociopathic killer!"

She jumped off the sofa and began sniffing my ankles.

So what are you saying? There's no ice cream?

No wonder dog people outnumber cat people two to one. (Well, if they don't, they should.)

For the second time that day, I got in the shower to wash away the memories of a most unpleasant experience. Not to mention the dirt and grime I'd picked up rolling around on the coast highway.

Then I got in my Frosty the Snowman pajamas (a Shopping Channel gift from my mom) and flopped into bed, where I slept like a rock until I was rudely awakened by a godawful pounding on my front door.

I sat up with a jolt. The sun was streaming in my window, and, according to my alarm clock, it was nearly noon.

"Jaine!" I heard Lance calling. "Open the door."

I hurried to the door, wondering what on earth could be the matter.

"What is it, Lance?" I muttered, as I flung the door open.

"There's somebody out front to see you."

"Who?"

"Looks like an exterminator," he said, hurrying back into his apartment.

"I didn't send for an exterminator."

I threw on my old chenille bathrobe, the one with the coffee stains in the shape of the Big Dipper, and stepped outside.

There, parked at the curb, was a Bug Blasters van, just like the one I showed up in for my lunch date with Andrew. I cringed, remembering how everyone on the restaurant patio had stared, goggle-eyed, at the 6-foot bug lying belly up on top of the van.

Was that Leonard parked at the curb, I wondered, the kindhearted guy who'd taken pity on me in my hour of need? Maybe there was a slump in the bug-blasting business and he was looking for work.

I started down the path to the street, when I saw somebody getting out of the van. But it wasn't Leonard.

Good heavens! It was Andrew!

Oh, crud. Why did I have to be wearing my Frosty the Snowman pajamas and that disgraceful coffee-stained robe?

Now he was heading up the path to my apartment, adorable as ever in khakis and a blue work shirt—carrying a bottle of champagne in one hand and a McDonald's take-out bag in the other.

I was speechless.

But Andrew wasn't.

"Who says I'd never show up for a date in an exterminator's van?"

And then he smiled a smile that could very well be responsible for global warming.

"Aren't you going to invite me in?"

No, absolutely not. I had to nip this romance in the bud. I had to ignore my emotions and Just Say No.

"Yes! Please! Come in!" were the words that actually came out of my mouth as I ushered him inside.

Okay, so I'm a pillar of tapioca. You try resisting those curls at the nape of his neck.

Prozac, who can smell a Quarter Pounder three counties away, came rocketing out of the kitchen and hurled herself at Andrew's ankles.

Hi, lover!

For the next hour or so, my apartment hummed with the sounds of belly rubs and contented purring.

And Prozac had a pretty good time, too.

Epilogue

Regan was arrested, of course. She and Hank both sang like canaries, and thanks to their damning indictments of one another, they'll be spending the next ninety-nine pilot seasons behind bars.

Good news about Allison. She swore off comedians forever and very sensibly fell in love with a fellow violinist at the symphony orchestra. As far as I know, they're happily married and waxing each other's bows in complete harmony.

Mrs. Spiro found out about Spiro's cheating ways and divorced the bum. She took everything in the settlement, including the Laff Palace, which she turned into a male strip club called The Body Shop. Holly works there as a barmaid and is dating one of the male strippers. (And so, incidentally, is Mrs. Spiro.)

Dorcas is back onstage, doing a comedy act about her time in jail. It's not all that bad. It's not all that good, either. But she's funnier than she used to be. And guess who her agent is? Manny Vernon. Right now he's got her booked at the Modesto Howard Johnson's, where she's the opening act for Elroy "Chuckles" Monahan.

You'll never believe this (I still don't!), but Pete found religion and gave up his porn collection. Last I heard, he was studying the Bible and teaching inner-city kids how to mix non-alcoholic drinks.

Needless to say, they never found my Corolla, which was all for the best. It was high time I stopped driving around town in a ten-year-old Corolla. Yes, thanks to the generous payment from my insurance company, I was able to trade all the way up to a nine-year-old Corolla.

I was so grateful to Crazy Dave for indirectly saving my life with his carcinogen-spewing car, I enrolled him in the Baklava-of-the-Month Club. (It's amazing what you can find on the internet.)

As for me, I'm sitting here in my sequined shorts set (I never did give it to charity), looking at my oil painting of dogs playing poker (I tried to give it away, but Goodwill wouldn't take it), musing on the nature of human relationships.

Andrew, of course, went back to Stuttgart. He says it won't be forever. But who knows? Maybe he'll come back and we'll reconnect. Or maybe he'll meet a Heidi Klum lookalike and I'll never see him again.

But no matter what happens, I'm glad he came into my life. I guess there's some truth to the old "'tis better to have loved and lost than never to have loved at all" gag.

Contrary to Prozac's prediction, I haven't checked into Heartbreak Hotel.

If anything, the whole episode has given me new hope for the future. I've come to realize that if a good guy like Andrew was attracted to me, there may, indeed, be Life After The Blob.

In fact, my romance with Andrew has inspired me to take up an ambitious new 1,200-calorie-a-day diet and exercise program. It's a very intense regimen, requiring a lot of dedication and willpower.

Which I intend to start the minute I finish my Eskimo Pie.

Catch you next time.